BILL, THE GALACTIC HERO

ON THE PLANET OF TEN THOUSAND BARS

Other Avon Books by
Harry Harrison

BILL, THE GALACTIC HERO

BILL, THE GALACTIC HERO
ON THE PLANET OF THE ROBOT SLAVES

BILL, THE GALACTIC HERO
ON THE PLANET OF BOTTLED BRAINS
with Robert Sheckley

BILL, THE GALACTIC HERO
ON THE PLANET OF TASTELESS PLEASURE
with David Bischoff

BILL, THE GALACTIC HERO
ON THE PLANET OF ZOMBIE VAMPIRES
with Jack C. Haldeman II

BILL, THE GALACTIC HERO

ON THE PLANET OF TEN THOUSAND BARS

HARRY HARRISON

AND DAVID BISCHOFF

Artwork by Mark Pacella

A Byron Preiss Book

AVON BOOKS  NEW YORK

BILL, THE GALACTIC HERO ON THE PLANET OF TEN THOUSAND BARS is an original publication of Avon Books. This work has never before appeared in book form. This work is a novel. Any similarity to actual persons or events is purely coincidental.

Special thanks to Nat Sobel, Henry Morrison, Chris Miller, David Keller, and John Betancourt.

DEDICATION: For John De Chancie

AVON BOOKS
A division of
The Hearst Corporation
1350 Avenue of the Americas
New York, New York 10019

BILL, THE GALACTIC HERO ON THE PLANET OF TEN THOUSAND BARS copyright © 1991 by Byron Preiss Visual Publications, Inc. Illustrations copyright © 1991 by Byron Preiss Visual Publications, Inc. Published by arrangement with Byron Preiss Visual Publications, Inc. Cover and book design by Alex Jay/Studio J.
Edited by David M. Harris
Front cover painting by Mark Pacella
Library of Congress Catalog Card Number: 91-91800
ISBN: 0-380-75666-8

First Avon Books Printing: September 1991

AVON TRADEMARK REG. U.S. PAT. OFF. AND IN OTHER COUNTRIES, MARCA REGISTRADA, HECHO EN U.S.A.

Printed in the U.S.A.

RA   10   9   8   7   6   5   4   3   2   1

BILL, THE GALACTIC HERO

ON THE PLANET OF TEN THOUSAND BARS

CHAPTER 1

THE POSTER ON THE WALL OF THE GAL-
actic Bureau of Investigation reception office depicted
a slavering seven-foot-tall lizardoid creature with a
human arm protruding repulsively from its fanged
jaws. The Chinger was a particularly obnoxious specimen of its breed, with razor-sharp scales gleaming
with sadistic highlights, its claws like sharpened sickles. The hideous creature's eyes glowed with satanic
evil, while saliva mixed with human blood trickled
down its green body to its muscle-bulging legs and
tail, wrapped modestly in chartreuse and lightning-
silver Danskins. Fierce, hypnotic evil glimmered in
the diamond-facet eyes. The thing looked like the
revolting result of a misprinted copy of AC/DC sado-
maso Comix, thought Sergeant Bill of Phigerinadon
II. Bill much preferred Furville Comix.

KILL A CHINGER FOR KRISHNA! declared the

paisley three-dimensional letters glowing and revolving like psychedelic barbershop posts.

Bill stared at the thing thoughtfully, while toothpicking from around his fangs the repulsive remains of this morning's sludge-in-a-bowl the galley had squeezed out to him.

"Pretty impressive, huh?" said the man behind the desk. A flickering holoslab labeled him as HERVIL SKIMMILQUETOAST. "That's the new design from the Emperor's Own Office of Accurate and Efficient Information." The guy was typical desk jockey meat, short, stupid and inefficient, with some sort of birth defect that made him look like a crocodile: green skin, bumps, pointy teeth and all. There were a lot of mutants in the galaxy, and as long as there was radiation, botched genetic gene-splicing and permits for Hollywoodworld producers to reproduce even more, there always would be. But that was okay, since you had to have people to run the Galactic Bureaucracy, and every other able-bodied son-of-a-bitch got shanghaied into the Troopers and paid the Emperor's credit debit. As long as they had a brain somewhere behind their alien eyes, could hunt and peck on their computer terminal and didn't short out communications wiring with their drool, they were prime paper-pusher material. "They say they used a real Chinger for photo-reference. Real arm, too. Bit of a scandal when it got et and they couldn't return it to the guy who loaned it—but that goes to show you. You can't trust a Chinger as far as you can blow them . . . I mean snow them . . ." He took his clawed finger out of a cavernous nostril, examined it unhappily, then pushed it back for a good root around. "Hmmm. Just what *do* I mean?"

There was just one thing that seemed to be normal

about this specimen from the Sears and Geekbuck catalog, observed Bill. And he leaned over the desk, giving his best Galactic-Trooper-makes-nice-nice grin. "Nice foot you got there, greeny," said Bill.

"Huh?" The bureaucrat ceased his nostril drilling, leaned forward in his chair, and blinked hard.

"I said, nice foot. Or I guess it would be, if you didn't have it in that shoe. Mind if I have a look?"

"Uhm . . . Mr. Trooper . . ."

"The name's Bill, buddy. Trooper Bill." Bill had to stop himself from grabbing the man by the throat and throttling him in a friendly drill instructor/recruiter love grip. This wasn't boot camp, but—and it was Bill's favorite game—a strange, warped variation on "Footsie."

"Trooper Bill. Did I hear you correctly? You want to look at my *foot.*"

"Yeah. I got this thing for feet. Call it a podiatry problem. Pedophilia, the shrink called it. And I got a little foot problem, too. It's irresistible—my little toe begins to itch—I can't control myself—arrgh!"

With no further ado, Bill lifted his leg up, plopped a naked foot upon the saurian bureaucrat's desk and scratched enthusiastically at his toe. And what a foot! It had twelve toes, gold toenails—and the skin was Royal Stuart tartan.

The guy's eyes bugged impressively, his jaw sagged—then snapped shut with an impressive clattering of fangs.

"Jumpin' Jupiter Juice! That's some foot. Might I be so presumptuous as to ask—what happened?"

"I'll tell you what happened. Completely by accident I shot the original one off on a planet called Veneria, that's what happened." He sniffed in self-pitying memory. "That's not easy to do, you know."

"But . . . but . . . if I may be so bold to ask—" the guy had an annoying whine to his voice, kind of like the sound a whoopee cushion makes on its last wheeze—"why?"

"Simple. It was the only way they'd let me off the planet. They had to ship me out because they were short of replacement feet. Eventually they just gave me a new foot and put me back on duty. But at least it was on a different planet."

"*That* foot?" said Herv.

"Not this one, idiot, another one. I've had so many feet I should be a mile by now. I've had so many feet I feel like a podiatrist's lab. I've had so many feet—"

The guy got a weird, frightened look on his face. "Oh, I get it," he simpered. "I've heard about you Troopers, locked up on those dreadnoughts for years without female companionship. Something has to snap—and often does, that's what I heard. So you've got this thing for feet."

Bill leaned over the desk with a menacing scowl. "Watch it, bowb. You calling me a prevert?"

"No, no, Trooper Bill," whinnied the clerk, recoiling, suddenly aware of those rolling trapezius, deltoid and triceps that bulged from Bill's frame like an inflated scuba suit. "Look, it's just not normal for me to, uh, show summoned agents my foot!" The guy made a conciliatory grin, but Bill was going to go for his throat anyway. He was interrupted by a squawk over the loudspeaker.

"*Skimmilquetoast! Is that the Trooper I sent for who is bellowing out his brains out there?*"

"Yes sir," said Herv, looking with trepidation up at Bill.

"Just a peek, huh? I promise I won't touch it!"

"*What are you two doing out there, playing 'Doctor'? Send the sphincter-muscle in!*" The intercom clicked off with a burst of static.

"C'mon, be a pal," said Bill. "I'll give you a credchit! I've got some Betelgeuse love beads with lots of juice. They're yours! How about a—"

"No. No, nothing. Here, if that's all you want, just look and then get the hell into the office before I lose my stupid job!" The clerk quickly took off his shoe and then his sock. He held up his pale green foot for Bill to see.

Bill sighed.

It was the most exquisite foot that Bill had ever seen.

From well-formed heels to perfect arches down to pedicured toenails painted pink, it looked like a Michelangelo sculpture or a Raphael painting of an angel. Albeit green. Bill's foot (on the other hand, or other foot) looked like garbage can modern.

"Nice foot," said Bill pleasantly. "Thanks."

"But what about your other one. Isn't that normal?"

Bill shook his head. "Flat. Broken toes. Corns on the cob. Usual Trooper's foot. You must be a very proud man. Cherish your foot, my friend." He wiped back a tear. "Well, I'd better see what this bowbhead wants."

Bill squared his shoulders and marched into the main office of J. Edgar Insufledor, deputy director of Anti-Chinger and Commupop Menace Operations of the GBI.

As soon as he marched in, he found himself directly in the sights of a Mark Thousand and Two Howitzer Laser Cannon. This piece of artillery sprouted from the Deputy Director's desk, which was made of riveted gray steel.

"Halt! Or be blown apart!"

Bill halted. He raised his hands in the time-honored signal for surrender, lack of weapons and requesting to go to the little boy's room. "It's just me. Trooper Bill. Loyal Trooper. Reporting as requested. Sir!"

"You sure you're not a Chinger spy!" growled the voice. Bill could see a grizzled crewcut grizzling up from behind the armorclad desk.

"No sir! Do I look green and seven feet tall, sir?" Bill knew full well from far too many personal experiences that far from being seven feet tall, Chingers were only seven inches tall. True, being from a high gravity world they were powerful little bug-eyed buggers, dangerous and crafty and killer poker-players. But he felt it best to play along with the Intergalactic propaganda crap, apparently even bought by its purveyors.

"Damned close! Could be a makeup job along with a tailectomy. True, you did make it in here through the cat-scan and failed the subliminal IQ exam. You're far too stupid to be a Chinger."

"Thank you. Sir!" Bill said, going into the usual Trooper barking mantra denoting respect, honor and the traditional raw hatred for your superiors.

"Very well, Bill." The laser cannon drooped noticeably and Bill felt a lot more comfortable. The man rose up from behind his armor shield, revealing features that looked like a cross between a warthog and a fire plug. A cigar the size of a starship escape pod stuck out from the side of his face. "Are you or have you ever been, in this life or a previous life, or have you ever even *wanted* to be or *thought about* being or might you *ever* be, in some future life in another dimension, a card-carrying member of the Commupop Party?"

Bill's thick eyebrows knitted. "Is this a trick question?"

The Commupop Party!

The Well-Read Menace!

There had been Commupops back on Phigerinadon II, Bill vaguely remembered, but they'd been wiped out by a Trooper raid when he was a little boy. He remembered that well because suddenly his Mom wouldn't give him cherry pop sickles any more, and because Mr. Leon Trotsky down the street was discovered hanging by his thumbs in the Town Square. This made Bill sad, because it was Mr. Trotsky who had given him the cherry pop sickles and had introduced him to Classix Comix Agitprop Bookskis and the whole idea of Comix, period. The real irony, said Mrs. Bill, was that Mr. Trotsky's real name was Fred Jones and he was just a fan of Russian history and literature, not a Commupop Party Member at all. But, as Bill would find out in his adult life, Galactic Troopers were trained in Boot Camp, not Book Camp, and they hung first and asked questions later. Bill's response was to ask his Mom if coprophilia had anything to do with loving policemen. Mom had muttered something about "damned intellectuals" and just let Bill go on reading his Comix after weeding out anything educational and threatening.

The Commupop Party, of course, was the abbreviation for the Community Popular Reading Party and had absolutely nothing to do with the Intergalactic Communist Party, or Saint Karl Marx. In fact, politically they were quite neutral and about as threatening to the Emperor's reign as, oh, his terminally backed-up toilet in his Rec Room on Wreckworld. However, the Emperor's rule being totalitarian and all, and the Communist Party being such a usual historical bugaboo, his Office of Paranoia and Disinformation fell upon the hapless Community Popular Reading Party like depleted uranium.

Thousands of hapless readers were sent to prison for reading the wrong books. A special committee was appointed to weed through the millions of books available to the general public and to ban the ones considered inappropriate to the general governmentally oppressed galactic citizen. To paraphrase the philosopher Santayana, those who do not know history are doomed to regurgitate it. The Emperor would have been better off just ignoring book readers. His persecution radicalized hundreds of thousands, who immediately became the revolutionaries the authorities feared they would be (albeit revolutionaries who, after a hard day of fire-bombing, went home to curl up with a nice thick book). Hence the creation of the Well-Read Menace, the Commupop Party.

"Trick question? Of course it's not a trick question, you idiot." The cigar bobbed obscenely and the man leaped up and hopped around, the fat on his squat body jiggling like warm Jell-O beneath his starched white shirt and black tie with Day-Glo polka dots. "You think I'm wasting my breath?"

Bill did exactly what he usually did when he faced a bureaucratic conundrum. "Look, I'm not going anywhere. The colonel told me to report here promptly at eleven hundred hours today for a special duty assignment. I ain't no Commupop Party Member, I'm a healthy reader of Blue-Blooded Galactic Comix and horny-porny comix—when I can get them—and proud of it. So while you figure out what you want with me, I'll just sit here and have some of the medicine that the doctor ordered me to take every hour."

He took out a medicine bottle that was really a flask of 100-proof rum (even Bill was smart enough not to take vodka into the GBI office), unscrewed the cap and tippled a good half of its contents, leaving his mouth open and making lots of noise.

Bill well knew that if he'd done such a thing in a Trooper office, he would have promptly been keel-hauled from the nearest deepspace freighter. However, this wasn't military business, it was GBI stuff and he was on loan.

Instead of being unhappy, however, the Director was sniffing the air ecstatically. "I can't believe it! You're just the man I need!"

"What? You want a hit too?" Bill offered the flask, already feeling the comforting kick of alcohol flattening his senses.

"Uhm . . . No, thank you, Trooper Bill. And now that my memory is refreshed and I reexamined my files, I remember why you're here. Sorry about the grilling. Knee-jerk reaction. If it's not the Chingers I must worry about, it's the damned Commupops. Bill, I got a very special assignment for you. The fate of the universe rests upon those considerable shoulders! Or something like that. Sit down, Bill, and let me turn off this damned machine here. Don't want to fry our most promising Special Agent, now, do we?"

Bill sat down, took another gurgle of drink, then tucked the flask back into his front pocket. It would have been a good idea for him to have put the top back on and to tuck it into his pocket bottom first, since he managed to spill about four ounces of primo rum onto his lap, staining his crotch and running chills down the hairy sides of his legs.

Bill shivered and grimaced, but managed to squelch an embarrassing shriek.

"Ha! Ha!" said the Director, pointing a stubby forefinger at the Trooper. "I saw that!"

"Uhm, uh, well—"

"No need to apologize, soldier. I myself get a *petite frisson* when I think of performing a special task for our glorious Emperor!" Overwhelmed by patriotism, the Director of the GBI swiveled and snapped a snappy straight-armed salute to the Illustrious Emperor, whose three-dee chinless and adenoidal picture hung prominently on the wall behind him. The Emperor's computerized image (the same Emperor whom Bill had very nearly almost met or at least perhaps got close to a stand-in in his youth) responded reflexively with a salute as well. Remarkable, thought Bill, gazing at the picture. They haven't fixed his strabismic eyes. It was nice to know that even an emperor had physical problems. Even as Bill regarded the stereoscopic image, the Emperor's right eye seemed to drift over of its own accord to spot Bill staring at him. But, of course, it *was* only a picture. Wasn't it? Of *course* it was. The Emperor was far too busy to spy on a lowly Trooper. Right? Paranoia was okay in its place, Bill thought. But *really!*

"Yeah, uh, right." Bill of course had no idea what *frisson* meant, but he never argued with, or attempted to understand, officers. "About the secret mission, sir." He didn't want to stay here too long, now that he'd dumped his liquor supply.

"The mission? Oh yeah. Right. The mission." J. Edgar Insufledor took a laser-pistol from a drawer and relit his monstrous cigar, boring a hole in the ceiling in the process. Bill could see many such holes in the ceiling, so he presumed that the upper office was either empty or a place used for private GBI executions. "Real simple, Bill. Barworld. Chingers." He spat the words out like he was expectorating cigar tips. "Time Continuum Vortex Nexus Locus Chasm!"

Bill's jaw dropped. "Barworld," he gasped. "D—d—did you say? *Bar*world?" He didn't hear anything else, just those beautiful, incredibly lovely words.

"I didn't say Bearworld and I didn't say Jarworld, Trooper. You heard me right. Barworld. That's where I'm sending you. That's where some trouble seems to be. There's rumors of some kind of Time/ Space disturbances there on the Transgalactic Seismo-Grundger, and our agents say the Chingers could well be at the bottom of the problem. And if they aren't, they're going to be! The Chingers have been looking for the secret key to Time for years, and do you know why, Bill?"

"*Bar*world?" Bill could only repeat like a litany. "*Bar*world!" Barworld, of course, was tantamount to a legend among Galactic Troopers! Perhaps it *was* a legend. But no Trooper ever got to discover the truth, since it was a resort world, and Troopers *never* got leave.

"I'll tell you why, Bill. Because those Chingers, they want to sneak up on us not only behind our backs—but the vermin want to sneak up *yesterday!* That's why."

"I volunteer!" said Bill, waving his black arm enthusiastically. "I'll go! I'll go."

"Those Chingers!" said J. Edgar Insufledor, foaming emphatically. "My duty in life is to rid this world of those God-damned infernal Galactic-grabbing Chingers!"

Abruptly, the door to one side of Bill crashed open. There, lumbering toward the Deputy Director, multiple arms thrashing and gigantic saurian face snapping snaggle-fanged jaws, was nothing less than a perfect representation of the Chinger in the poster! Minus, of course, the human arm in its mouth. Apparently that had long since been digested, and the Chinger was in need of fresh human meat.

Wait a moment, thought Bill in the back of his mind. Chingers don't get this big. His eternal adversary Bgr the Chinger (who had come into his life as the lackeyish recruit Eager Beager) was only a fraction over seven inches tall!

Still it was difficult to argue with a roaring lizard alien, hands full of knives and guns, and eyes full of the promise of nothing but hard, hot death.

Fortunately, though, the giant Chinger was headed straight for J. Edgar Insufledor, not giving Bill a moment's pause. The Deputy Director was ready for him, though. "C'mon you piece of deep space sludge. Come and get it, planet grunge!" The Deputy Director pulled out a duplicate of an antique prehistoric vintage G-man style submachine gun and aimed at the charging beastie.

"Grrrumargggggggggg!" roared the savage space beast. Bill had *never* heard a Chinger utter this particular outcry before. He'd heard Chingers curse in Greek, Swahili, Russian and of course their own hissing and eructing language. Still and all, this particular specimen uttered the cry with such complete conviction that Bill took its word for it. Never one to question the wisdom of the hasty retreat in such brutal matters as these, Bill nonetheless immediately saw that an exit, albeit hasty, would put him in the path of submachine bullets. Instead, he jumped behind the overstuffed couch.

"Take this, you foul creature!" cried J. Edgar Insufledor. When the beast was just a yard away, the Director fired. The submachine chattered and bullets chunk-a-chunked into the lizard's green hide, kicking up divots of flesh. The Chinger sprayed blood like a lawn-watering device. It was pushed back a full foot, its guns knocked spinning from ruined claws. A single knife remained in its possession as it screeched sanguinely and leaped for the director again, slashing his weapon like molten lightning.

Bill cringed helplessly behind the couch. He didn't know what was going on here, but it was certainly a great deal deadlier than Denubian tiddlywinks.

"Aha! You enjoy eating hot lead!" the Deputy Director said calmly through gritted teeth, his still-fuming cigar sticking up like an exclamation point. "Then have some more, Chinger!"

J. Edgar Insufledor shot off the knife hand and then put another clip of bullets in the Chinger's chest. The creature went down like a sack of bloody potatoes, spasming and slashing still at its prey. Jaws snapping, it pulled itself toward the Director.

J. Edgar Insufledor threw aside his Thompson. "This is a job for Deathdealer," he said, a smile crinkling the corners of his mouth and eyes. From behind his desk he pulled out a two-handed claymore sword. "Okay Chinger. Let me show you how a real man deals with a bowby alien."

J. Edgar stepped forward and proceeded to hack open the Chinger's skull with untrammeled ferocity.

Green blood geysered everywhere, splattering on the walls and, when he ventured a peek, into Bill's eyes. By the time he cleared his vision the Chinger was literally chopped into nuggets on the carpet, oozing and stone-cold dead. Only the tip of its tail flickered about like a snake whose head has been lopped off.

"Bill!" cried J. Edgar Insufledor. Somehow in the struggle, the top of his shirt had unbuttoned, revealing a clump of manly chest hair. He put a possessive foot on the largest chunk of the creature and seemed to pose like a big game hunter. "Some tussle, eh? Wise of you to take cover! These varmints are mean mothers!"

Hesitantly, Bill rose up from his hiding place. "You wouldn't have a shot of whiskey hiding anywhere about, would you?"

"Nope. Don't touch the stuff. Harms my precious Puritan bodily fluids. But your taste for it and your unusual record of service is why the GBI wants you!"

Skimmilquetoast stuck his head into the office. "Oh dear. Thank Mithra, sir! You got it. The assassin Chinger just charged through, slapped me aside and headed straight in for YOU!" The man turned to Bill and gave him a broad wink. Bill, nonplussed, could only gape. "Yet, once again, you have saved yourself and the day, to say nothing of the welfare of the Galaxy!"

The Director grunted. "All in a day's work. Just get a crew in to clean this mess up. And oh—mount the usual trophy with its head, eh Skimmilquetoast? Makes for a wonderful dinner conversation piece!"

"Yes, *sir!*"

"Now then, Bill. You will be dispatched to Barworld with complete instructions surgically subcutaneously planted in your left earlobe. However, although you certainly enjoy your drink, it has been determined that you are not sufficiently—er—alcoholic, not to mince words, for the full cover we need." Insufledor sucked on his cigar, then scooped up a folder drenched in lizard blood and handed it to Bill. "This contains the information on the most alcoholic Trooper still serving in the Galactic Troopers. He shall be your companion. The first part of your mission shall be to find this man, sober him up long enough to brief him, then bring him back. We will then send you off to Barworld to see into this very important matter."

"Yes, *sir!*" he snapped ecstatically, visions of countless bottles dancing in his head.

He didn't want to louse up a chance to go to Barworld! It was a Trooper's fantasy, and one of Bill's few heartfelt ambitions.

"Skimmilquetoast. Show this fine Trooper out. Oh, and get a move on getting those janitors in to clean this up. Tell security to be a little more on their toes, eh? Can't do their work for them *all* the time, now, can I?"

"Yes, sir! Trooper, would you please be so kind as to aid me in hauling this disgusting thing from the Director's office so as not to disgust him any further?" The assistant picked up one of the feet and nodded toward the other. Bill shrugged and did so, bringing his ample strength to bear. Outside the office, the Director's door slammed shut. The Chinger's arm got stuck in a fishhook-coated modernist wire sculpture. Bill tugged harder and the Chinger's leg, half-ripped off with bullet wounds anyway, came off trailing hunks of lizard flesh, veins and wires.

Wires?

Still, Bill half expected as much. There was something fishy about that lizard.

"Best idea the Director ever had—and Bureau-psych concurs. He deals every day with the threats to the welfare of the Empire from his desk but he never gets to actually kill anything. So, every once in awhile, we throw in a cyborg Commupop or Chinger to keep him on his toes. Old man *loves* it! He'll have a smile on his face for at least a week—and will maybe leave off the ritual staff-whipping for a while!"

Bill tossed the leg down and wiped his hands on his pants. "You got to give me the details on this Trooper I'm supposed to go get, and then point me to the nearest MacRotgut's. I feel like a nice MacDTs for a liquid lunch."

"Sure, Sarge." He handed Bill a folder and a watch with a complicated gadget on it. "Quantum sub-space radio for top-secret communications if you got any problems or questions. Oh, and by the way. Best to keep that foot out of your mouth, eh?"

Bill was tempted to put the foot somewhere else a good deal more satisfactory than his mouth, but he decided that since he was going to have to rely on this bowb-brain for information for a long time, he'd better not do anything quite so enthusiastic.

He went for that drink he'd been promising him-self, hoping to encounter no cyborg Chingers or Commupops along the way.

CHAPTER **2**

BILL WAS IN COMPLETE TOTAL AND UT-
ter bliss.

Well, not precisely complete. Or utter. What little
that remained unobliterated in the way of deep human
emotions in Bill twinged ever so slightly, lifted their
heads feebly from the abyssal depths of depression
and, like frail shoots in April lured on by the siren
promise of spring, began to flower with weensy buds
of hope.

Barworld!

For all the years—it seemed like centuries—that he
had served in the Troopers, in the grueling grapple
of combat and the even worse conditions in boot
camp on both sides of the boot, stationed on pus-
tulating planets and in stagnant starships that made
him want to flip his cookies just thinking about them,
doomed to a dark bleak existence of hard beds, hard

heads and *no* hard creds... for all those years, the concept of R&R was strictly *verboten* in the Service; leave had long since left. A Trooper's duty was to serve his Emperor twenty-four and a half hours a day, three hundred and sixty-six days a year—and that under the shrunken Galactic Disgustan Calendar, only half as long as the Augustan. The only joys in a Trooper's life were two-credit/two-minute ladies of the morning (the ladies of the evening were far too expensive), and in smoking de-tarred and de-nicotinized cigarettes (in the hopes that they would shorten their miserable, wasted lives in this dubiously pleasurable fashion), Comix (albeit jam-packed with subliminal loyalty reinforcement, like Chingers and Commupops generally being the bad guys) and, of course, booze. However, even the simple joys of Trooper life tended to be watered-down and tepid. The doxies were old and bored and tended to use their creds as down payments on powered wheel-chairs. The cigarettes were made of dried tobacco stems, since the real stuff was reserved for the officer classes. Comix doubled for toilet paper; the ultimate literary criticism.

And the booze...

To say that the booze was the pits was to insult underarms and coal mines all over the known universe. It tended to be repulsively flavored, cheaply manufactured ethanol, rumored to be from Under-takerworld, so that in lieu of alcohol embalming fluid was often used.

Bill hadn't known the difference for a long time, but whenever during his various adventures he'd actually tasted some real beer, some real wine, and most of all genuine unsynthetic whiskey, gin and rum, he knew that he wanted to dedicate his life to finding a world where he could sample again the fruits of this delicious alcoholic vine.

Such a world, it was whispered in the darkness, was Barworld.

And the Galactic Feds were actually sending him there!

That was if he could only find this guy whose dossier had been given him in that vanilla folder. (He knew it was vanilla and not manila because he'd gotten drunk at his liquid lunch and eaten it.)

As it happened, the Trooper that Bill had been dispatched to find—Lieutenant Hardtack Brandox, Jr.—was at this moment right here on the same planet as Bill, the main location of Galactic bureaucratic matters and center for the manufacture of women's underwear, Drawerworld.

A good deal of red tape, filing of requests and crossed communications later (to say nothing of stop-offs at bars and latrines to research Brandox's famous drinking habits and, perhaps, maybe a snort or two for himself), Bill found Lieutenant Brandox's squadron to be on Jinx Ether Force Base.

"Make it fast," snarled Captain Quarterpounder, looking up suspiciously at Bill from a mountain of paperwork. "Lieutenant Brandy? What a boozer. Sweats pure ethyl. But you're too late, bowb-brains. Should have been here a day earlier. He's just been reassigned to Some Godforsaken Planet."

"Which planet?"

"Some Godforsaken Planet, bowb—don't you hear very well? That's the name. That's what they call it. Deathworld 69 to be more specific. One of the several hundred slaughterhouses of combat between humans and the Chingers, along with the rest of the filthy ETs in the universe, Ahura Mazda rot their alien green bones!"

"Well, perhaps you can call him back. I am on official business." Bill showed him the ID bracelet that the GBI had given him, strapped on the wrist under his communicator.

"Tough termites, Trooper. That bit of bureaucratic bowb means nothing here. Brandox is well on his alcohol-sodden way to the lift-off fields."

The captain gloomily examined a chronometer. Satisfied that the chrono was still metered, he examined the standard issue Trooper Clock bearing the scowling face of the Beloved Emperor. "Should be blasting off in about two hours. If you move your butt you might just catch it." He grinned with cheerful sadism. "Or you can maybe go along for the ride. I hear that Deathworld 69 is really *in* this year for suicidal tours of duty."

"No thanks. I've got something to *live* for!" said Bill enthusiastically.

The captain eyed him suspiciously. "Something *wrong* with you, Trooper? You're supposed to die doing your duty. Come home with your shield or on it. You know the bowb."

"No sir! I mean yes, sir!" Bill realized with horror that he'd almost spilled the beans about being on his way to Barworld—a definite no-no, since not only was the mission top secret but the captain would probably shoot him from sheer jealousy. "I think it was just a spasm of pure joy from beholding our dear Emperor's face there smiling away on the bulkhead."

"Yeah? Well, stow it when you are around here, buddy. It's bowb-your-buddy month here on Drawerworld and we've only got one month per year. Understand?"

Bill sneered, showing his fangs in his best DI manner. He saluted with both his right hands. "Yes sir!"

He trotted off for the takeoff fields to find Lt. Brandox before the starship made its lift-off.

The Happy Trails Takeoff fields were about two hours away by grav-car, but Bill, through breakneck speed, high-reflex steering and the sacrifice of a few dogs, cats, a little old lady and a second lieutenant, managed to make it to them in just a little over an hour and a half.

As always, when he approached the mighty Imperial launching pads Bill gasped an appreciative gasp or two at the sight of the towering behemoth starships reaching imperially toward the sky, their shiny impervium sparkling in the sunlight, the silvery needles of their bows pointed upward toward challenge and adventure.

Then, as usual, he experienced a depressing mood swing as he was admitted by the checkpoint guard past the ceremonial holo-facade of these imaginary vessels into the grungy and smoggy reality of the true Imperial takeoff fields. Greasy smoke poured up from cracks in the ground. The smell of diesel fuel and sulfur permeated the air. Blackened technicians trucked around in dilapidated service vehicles looking like recently nuked worker ants. There were maybe twenty starships in various states of disrepair rising up from the ground like twisted mushrooms in a bed of mold. Their skins were pitted by the craters of interstellar dust, spattered with the bird droppings of countless worlds.

The question was, which one was Brandox's?

Bill stopped a gray-skinned Trooper wearing corporal's stripes on his eyepatch and inquired.

"Deathworld 69? That's like a really hard question. We've got maybe three starships getting ready to heave up mightily through the atmosphere. Hard to tell them apart." The corporal, Bill noticed, had the telltale scars on his forehead of a jobotomy. That was why he wasn't being shipped off himself; he'd probably been a trouble-maker or attempted to go AWO (there was no AWOL or Absent WithOut Leave in This Bowb's Army, since "leave" was a foreign concept). A jobotomy was like a lobotomy, only they stuck a little programmed computer in the place where there used to be about half the gray matter; it kept the victim in line and gave him a preprogrammed duty. The corporal sighed. "Wish I could go with them into glorious battle. Alas, I am but a ground jockey. Gotta serve my Empire here amidst the dirt and gravity. But like the Emperor says, 'They also serve who stand and wait!'"

"Wait? Wait for what? Just knock off that pseudo-romantic bowb and tell me which ship it is."

The corporal just grinned, glassy-eyed.

"Never mind," said Bill. "I'll find it myself."

It shouldn't be too hard, Bill muttered to himself. Starships about ready to take off from the ground look a lot different from the moribund, inactive sort. Like their ports were closed: good clue! And they shake around like a pent-up volcano, spurting steam from their seams and generally looking like water heaters about to blow. Hell, some of them *did* blow, instantly killing all aboard and anyone in the immediate vicinity. In the past, with atomic drives, there had been nuclear explosions that destroyed whole cities. This was why atomic drives were no longer allowed for lift-off use. Steam catapults hurled them into the air, then chemical booster rockets were

used. At least when these blew up, they did so dis-
creetly in the atmosphere where no high-level officers
were around.

It didn't take long for Bill to find a likely candidate
for the Rocket Ship Most Likely To. There was a
particularly noisy and noisome bucket of bolts in
midfield that was vibrating like a teakettle at full boil.
Its engines were building up to an excited white-hot
state of excitement, and lights were spinning wildly
everywhere. However, since a large gangplank was
still extended and a noncom was standing at its base
with a clipboard and an atomic ballpoint, Bill thought
maybe there were still a few minutes left until igni-
tion.

"Hey buddy, no way are we going to fit that grav-
car you're driving into the BEELZEBUB!" said the
noncom, a beefy sergeant with a chip on his shoulder.
It was a corn chip, apparently from lunch, but Bill
didn't have the time or the patience to tell the guy
how stupid it looked.

"I'm not shipping the car, I—"

"Then get it the hell outta here. To one of the
satellite lots. Take a right at the abandoned second-
stage thruster, and a left at the graveyard till you see
the pile of rusty rockets. Move it."

"Look, is this rocket going to Some Godforsaken
Planet?"

Sgt. Porky looked at him like he was from Hay-
seedworld. "Well of *course* it's going to some godforsaken planet. They all do."

"No, that's the *name* of the place. Some Godforsaken Planet."

"Look, buddy, if you ain't got a name, I can't help
you." A noisy blast of steam drowned out his voice.

"What?" said Bill.

"What's on Second Baseworld," said the guy.

"Who?"

"Who's on Firstworld. Plays shortstop for the Yankee Imperialists. Every sports-loving Trooper knows that, bowbhead." His eyes squinted up with suspicion. "You a Chinger spy or something?"

Bill refrained from killing him on the spot. Teeth grinding, he shoved his official Galactic Bureau of Investigation documents under the corporal's nose.

"Geez. A Fed. Sorry, you excellency. How can I serve you?" said the fat man, suddenly shiveringly penitent.

"Where is this starship going?"

"Deathworld 69, sir. In the Missionary Position nebula."

"That's Some Godforsaken Planet!"

"Yes sir, it certainly is." The sergeant nodded his head emphatically. "It's real hell. Troopers who go there never come back. Alive. Why's the GBI sending you there? Some kind of special mission?"

Bill sighed off his frustration. "No, I'm not going there. I need to get a guy in this ship who has been dispatched there. We need him. You got an officer in there name of Brandox?"

The guard consulted his clipboard. "Yeah. Here we go, sir. Brandox. He's aboard. But we've only got five minutes till we seal the port. Wouldn't do to have a starship lift off into the near vacuum with its barn door hanging wide open, now would it?"

"One more joke and you are dead. Stop all lift-off procedures instantly."

"I can't!" He wailed, vibrating with fear. "You stop the countdown on one of these antique models, they blow up. Energy-saving measure, Emperor's own orders."

"I gotta get in there and get that guy out before the doors close, then. Right. A Trooper's gotta do what a Trooper's gotta do." Namely, get this alcoholic officer out of there so they could both go to Barworld. Bill parked the grav-car (on the check-in sergeant's foot at first, which cost a scream of grief and a wasted forty-five seconds) then galloped up the starship ramp.

That the BEELZEBUB was a "Meat Runner"—Trooper argot for a vessel that dragged the detritus of the military ranks to their dooms—was immediately made apparent by the profound odor de Trooper that met Bill's nose upon entering the hold. The starship itself was clearly an old freighter pressed into service not only long past its prime but well past its expiration date. Its welds were strained, its wiring leaking volts and the whole thing vibrated like a Spican wartdog in rut. Bill slapped his way through a number of hanging cables and plumbing lines, his nose twitching at the visible fug of the interior. The autolifts were welded immobile with rust, so Bill had to climb a series of ladders.

Finally, he reached a large, dark chamber only dimly lit by the starship's reactor core and a few candles.

"Is there a Lieutenant Brandox Junior in here!"

Groans. The clank of tin cups, the slosh of chamber pots, the smell of stale bread and beans, the clank of chains. Dim forms moved in the shadows.

"Lieutenant Brandox Junior didja say?" came a groan.

"That's right," said Bill hopefully.

"Ain't me!"

"Not me!"

"I ain't Brandox, that's for sure!" came the growls in response.

Damn! Time was running out. The doors were going to close on this thing any minute, and Bill would be trapped on the way to Deathworld 69, never to return!

"Well, who the bowb is!"

"He's up in the *really* nasty part of the ship. He's in solitary along with some other bowbheads."

"Wonderful." Bill didn't question the concept of a shared solitary cell not only because he didn't have time, but because this was a typical Trooper paradox. Bill just scrambled up another ladder into a truly filthy section of the craft, if slightly better lit by the even more radioactive core. That was okay, thought Bill. He'd been getting a bit pale lately and he could use a tan.

"Lieutenant Brandox!" He cried. "Junior."

"Hey pal!" slurred a voice. "Shat's me! What's shup?"

Bill turned. There against a wall was a true wreck of a Trooper holding a liter bottle of clear liquid. His nose was red and his eyes were so bloodshot they looked as though there were no whites in them at all, just pupil and veins. The odor of pure ethanol wafted over to Bill. For the first time in his entire life, Bill was offended by the smell of drink. The overall stink of the place must be getting to him.

"Wanna drink?"

"Not right now. Take a look at this." Bill waved his GBI identification before the unseeing eyes. "C'mon, lieutenant. We gotta move—but fast."

"You betcha—but gotta bring my bottle."

"Do it. That's why we want you."

Bill dragged the drunk after him; he smelled like

bargain night in the Dingbat Distillery. Bill took a deep breath and decided maybe to leave off the booze a while, just so that he'd be really primed for Barworld. But even as Brandox took an unsteady step, there was a jarring clang and he was pulled back into an abrupt sitting position.

"Urp!" He said. "Forgot. Little problem." He jerkily indicated the tungsten bar around his chest, chained to the bulkhead by impervium, the hardest metal known. "You got a thermal lance?"

"Two minutes until closing of hatch!" rasped a fiendish voice on the loudspeaker.

Bill squealed. He gave a feeble tug on the chain, but he knew it would be no good, and he sure as hell didn't have time to look for a hacksaw—which even if he found it would be about as useful as an umbrella in a meteor shower.

"Sorry, Brandox. Looks like you're stuck here. Oh well, they say that Some Godforsaken Planet has nice sunsets this time of year."

"Then I hope I get there after Deathworld 69!" said Brandox. "And I hope they've got good Margaritas." The drunken lieutenant promptly passed out.

"Just as well," muttered Bill to himself as he searched for the exit. "I'd have to *carry* this lush to Barworld."

Bill was just going to have to report that Lt. Brandox was unavailable for Special Mission Duty.

He found the ladder and crawled down it.

He made his way through the murky hold, anxious to get out of this Trooper's hellhole, searching for the exit. So anxious was Bill, in fact, that he did not notice the rusty chain slung along the floor at ankle level. He charged straight into it and went sprawling into the wall. *Snap* went the chain. However, his hardened Trooper reflexes (and hardened Trooper head) prevented him from tumbling in unconsciousness after his noggin met some metal. As he looked up blearily, looking for the exit, he was still quite aware that unless he got his face through that door in under two minutes, his butt was going to get shipped to Deathworld 69.

Which was, of course, Some Godforsaken Planet any bowbing way you sliced it.

There it was! The way out!

A form reared before Bill, blocking the exit. "Outta the way, you mother bowber!" shouted Bill politely. "I gotta get off this tub!"

The form solidified into a shaggy, bearded man covered with a mass of rags. "Slowly I turn," the man rumbled with a deep, ominous voice. "Step by step... inch by inch...." The man lifted his leg, from which an old broken chain depended. "I'm free! I don't believe it! You've *freed* me! I've been in this starship, forgotten, for years! And you've freed me! How ever can I thank you?"

"You can just move it! I've gotta get down this ladder!"

A loudspeaker rattled. "One minute till closing of hatch. Next stop: Some Godforsaken Planet!"

"Oh no! That's Deathworld 69! There is death, only death there!" The man fell to his knees, blubbering miserably before Bill. "Oh, please good buddy! Please take me with you!"

"Get outta my way!"

"Please sir! I'll give you the Secret to the Universe! I know the meaning of Life itself!"

"Look, butt-head, I don't care if you've got the keys to the Captain's liquor cabinet. This boat's gonna blow soon, and I'm not going to be on it!"

"I'm not lying!"

"Thirty seconds to hatch closing. . . . Last chance for flight insurance. A mere ten million credits per head. Twenty-nine seconds. . . ."

Bill was starting to panic. He gave the guy a hard, quick shove. The ragged man fell backward, rolled and fell straight back and down the hatchway. He grabbed at the ladder which clattered and jerked—

—and then collapsed, cutting Bill off from egress.

Bill stared, horrified.

"Twenty-five seconds. Kiss your Trooper butts good-bye!" came the reassuring rasp of the loudspeaker.

Now, Bill had been in the deep end before, so he knew exactly what worked best in such clearly difficult situations.

Total and complete, mind-destroying panic!

Not thinking about the immediate danger, only thinking about getting stuck on a planet like Veneria again, Bill screamed shrilly and dived headfirst down the hatchway.

He landed surprisingly softly.

"Ooof!" came a cry. "Ouch!" came another. "Hey buddy! You wanna get off us! Like it's not bad enough we're doomed, we gotta get landed on by some fat goofball!"

Fortunately he'd landed on a communal Trooper mattress, complete with communal Troopers.

Bill would have taken exception to the word "fat" but the loudspeaker was reminding everybody smugly that they had exactly ten—no, *nine* seconds till the hatch closed.

Bill scrambled off the mattress, impeded by various Trooper limbs and faces. "Hey bud, why don't you stick around!"

"Yeah! We could use some company."

Bill distributed a few punches and broke loose of the tangle. He struggled toward the smudgy bar of light that was the hatchway.

"Four seconds. Two seconds."

"Hey wait a minute!" screamed Bill. "You missed 'Three seconds.' "

"Three seconds?" said the intercom voice. "Did I miss three seconds, Madge? I could have sworn I hit three. Oh well, Three seconds. One seconds."

"What about two?" screeched Bill.

"Dammit. I said two! Look buddy, you want me to have to do a playback for you? I can, you know. We've got the equipment!"

The hatchway was right in front of him.

The door was beginning to close. Bill remembered the hellish jungle, the sweat, the horror, the pain of having to shoot off his own foot to get off the last deathworld he had been on. Spurred on by this vision, he leaped forward and through the closing door at the last possible microsecond.

He rolled down the ramp, huffing and heaving, coming to a stop by two pair of feet. One pair was shod, the other bare and calloused and unbelievably filthy.

"Hey, guy," said the guard. "This guy Brandox?"

Bill was about to say, "Hell no!" However, he was halted by a pair of bright eyes beneath the herbiage staring down at him imploringly. Bill was going to say "Hell no!" anyway because he was plenty put-out by his near escape, but something, he didn't know what, a little nagging voice of compassion, perhaps some submicroscopic scrap of conscience and compassion lingering in a dusty corner of his brain from his pre-Trooper days, stopped him. Or maybe it was just heartburn.

"Yeah. That's him. He's coming with me."

"Well, I suggest you get in your grav-car and get the hell outta here because these things go off in an explosion that cinders living things for miles around." The man then shot out of there, running hell bent for leather. Whatever that means.

Blinking with joy, the man that Bill had inadvertently saved scrambled eagerly into the back seat of the grav-car.

Grumpily, Bill leaped into the driver's seat and gunned the anti-grav repulsors. "I don't know why I'm doing this. I just don't know," he said as he raced away.

"You won't be sorry, Bill. I promise you," said the man. He was starting to speak much plainer now. And he sounded positively familiar.

Seconds later Bill felt the heat of the rocket taking off. Light flared all about him and the grav-car bucked. He kept on going and he heard the BEELZEBUB roaring away, cutting through the atmosphere toward its dreadful destination.

When he thought it was safe, Bill stopped and turned to his passenger. "Okay, bowb-breath. That's as far as you go. I got better—"

The back seat was empty.

The guy was already gone.

Bill shrugged, but his hackles were raised with a chill. Where'd the guy go?

A chill breeze of superstitious fear stirred the short hairs on his neck, chilled his large intestine as well. A ghost of Trooper past. He jammed down on the throttle.

CHAPTER 3

"TROOPER BILL?"

Bill looked up groggily, seeing everything through beer-colored glasses.

"Trooper Bill? Can you read me? Over?"

Bill realized that the reason his glasses were beer-colored was because he'd passed out in a spaceport bar. Everything was agreeably dark and cozy and soft, as good bars usually are. Except for his eyes, which ached because he was facedown on top of two glasses of beer. He grabbed them and pulled his head free with sucking-popping sounds and looked around blearily. There were only a few other patrons, two of whom were zonked out in pools of liquor on the floor, in good Trooper tradition.

"Grundgle?" said Bill.

"Look at your two-way sub-space super-quantum radio, idiot!" said the insistent voice from the general direction of his wrist. Bill blearily examined the device and noted J. Edgar Insufledor's ugly image peering out accusingly. "Listen up, Bill. We've decided that your failure to produce Lt. Brandox was all to the good. We've reached the inescapable conclusion that you'll have to do for alcoholic cover. You seem to have a natural talent for it."

Bill tried to respond, but a mind-destroying belch punctuated by a hiccup got in his way.

"Excellent. We see you've already been working hard in preparation. However, in this situation, we've decided that you'll need a companion agent. A top agent of ours. He's sitting right beside you at this moment. His name is Elliot Methadrine, G-man. Say hi to your new partner, Elliot, and show how friendly and forthright a good honest Emperor's G-man can be."

The man standing there turned around and extended a friendly hand. "Gee! Nice to meet you, Trooper Bill. Gee—this is going to be a great mission isn't it? Barworld! I bet I can do some wizard chin-ups there. Ho, ho!"

Bill frowned with consternation while he blinked to clear his beer-blurred vision. *Gee.* Where had he heard that expression before? Or had he ever heard it before? Maybe that's why they were called G-men. Bill was still vibrating with expectancy at the notion of going to Barworld, as well as twanging with horror in memory of his close escape from the BEELZEBUB. So, vibrating and twanging, he reached out unsteadily and shook the newcomer's hand.

Elliot Methadrine had a fresh-scrubbed face, blond slicked-back hair, baby-blue eyes, and was generally so clean-cut and wholesome that he didn't even have fuzz in his navel. He was garbed in a freshly cleaned pin-striped suit and wore a solid baby-blue tie—it exactly matched his eyes—held in place by a gold pin. By his side was a violin case.

"Bludga," Bill gasped, his speaking apparatus still not in gear.

"Gee. We're going to really thwart those rotten Chingers, right Trooper Bill!" Elliot Methadrine bobbed his head with vacuous enthusiasm. "You'll see. Together we'll be a top-flight team. I sincerely trust that the operation on your earlobe wasn't too strenuous or painful."

Now that his attention was drawn to it, Bill realized that his ear did ache. Or maybe just coming out of the alcoholic fog reconnected his nervous system. Bill's reddened, swollen ear began to throb dully and he realized that he had a nebula-sized headache as well. He ordered an aspirin, a shot of novocaine, a Sobering Effect pill and a beer. He dumped the pills and the novocaine in the beer, shot glass and all, and chugalugged it.

"*Yarrrgh!*" Bill screamed as the concoction exploded in his stomach and sent shockwaves through his system. In an instant he was clearheaded and sober. And hating it. The image of his employer on his wrist spoke again.

"Excellent to see you working together. I have pressing matters to attend to now, as always, so you guys get to know each other. All the instructions are in your ear, Bill. And if you get to kill any Commupop rabble-rousers along the way, all the better! Over and out."

"Gee—isn't Mr. J. Edgar Insufledor just the best boss ever?"

"Buy me another drink, Elliot. Get one for yourself. We might as well get to know each other, huh?"

"Yeah, sure, I guess. Bartender—the same again for my friend—"

"Heavy on the novocaine?" the barman asked.

"No, bowb-head. I'm sober now so it's back to the booze. Large beer with a whiskey chaser."

"And I'll have a root beer. Heavy on the root!"

"Wait a minute! They're sending me to Barworld with a teetotaler. What kind of cover is *that* going to be, for Krishna's sake?"

"Oh—Gee—I drink, Bill. Fact, they say I've got a regular holo-leg!"

"Hollow leg, you mean. So how come you're not drinking with me? Couple guys get to know each other proper, they should clink a couple of glasses. And I don't mean glasses of root beer."

"Gee," said Elliot Methadrine, nodding as though Bill had said something very profound and wise. "Okay. I'll have a beer."

"There. That's better. So we get to know each other, I'll tell you the story of my life. I was born. When I grew up I got tricked into joining the Troopers by a guy named Deathwish Drang, whose fangs these were." He thumbed one of the protruding teeth in question. It resonated like a tuning fork in B-sharp. "I've been dragged through hell and back, spilled a lot a beer, broken a few hearts and a few heads and feel immensely sorry for myself. And I'm gonna die. Probably soon, but hopefully not before this mission is over. How about you?"

"Gee—what patriotism. What gritty philosophy! What a hard-boiled man! You are an inspiration to us all."

Suspicion filled Bill again. What this geezer said sounded like the ripe-old bowb. But then the barkeep refilled his glass, distracting him. Bill relaxed and drank deep.

"So go on, tell me *your* story, partner."

"Sure!" The kid wiped the foam off his lips with a sleeve of his coat. "Not much to tell, really. But I'll give her a go!"

Elliot, as he explained, had been born to be a G-man. Indeed, he had been born on a one-G world, on a planet that circled around a sun called G-Whizz. G-world had been colonized by law officers and Government men and Secret Service agents of the pre-Empire days, during an era of uncharacteristic peace in human history. Having not much in the way of violent peacekeeping to do, the lawmen emigrated to an already colonized world then populated by racists, libertarians and proto-fascists who were fleeing from justice. They had set up their own judicial system, declared most activities on the planet illegal, other than the sale of guns, and promptly began to enforce the new law, with as much bloodshed and gratuitous violence as possible. When the G-men arrived it was warfare at first sight. When they began to lose, the desperate populace began to import criminals, mafiosi and drug dealers from around the galaxy to help them battle this G-men menace, which pleased the law enforcers immensely. A bright entrepreneur set up a documentary channel covering G-world for Galactic cable and it was an instant number-one ratings hit. So much so that within a generation planets began to emulate the action-filled place, and Poof! There went the galactic peace. The Empire was established to restore peace, even if force was needed. They would be saved even if they had to be destroyed. Which sounded familiar. Soon humans on all systems began plugging and zapping one another again, which ended in the ongoing establishment of the Empire once and for all. But after peace broke out, the generals and admirals grew restless. So they welcomed with open arms the Chinger menace that loomed ahead of them. Of course it wasn't a real menace since the Chingers had never heard of war. This had never stopped the military before. A little adroit propaganda and the battle was on! Now they could turn their energies to destroying aliens and giving each other medals.

Elliot Methadrine was from a long line of G-men specializing in enforcing prohibition on G-world, while running breweries, wineries and distilleries on the side. (Hence Elliot's built-up tolerance for alcohol.) He'd been trained in G-world Academy, was a top marksman with lasers, blasters and bullet-firing weapons, knew ten different forms of martial arts and could make a *mean* fried tofu burger. His hobbies included bird watching, knitting, collecting UN-TOUCHABLE COMIX (a Hindu publication, one of the few religious Comix permitted) and he was a part-time executioner one weekend a month in the Executioner Reserves, to help his cousins get through law school.

Bill listened to all this bowb with immense disinterest, nodding over his beer. By this time, they were through a few drinks. Bill was markedly drooped on the seat, but Elliot still looked chipper and alert despite a steady downing of powerful beverages.

The male bonding was almost complete.

"Okay. Sounds good," said Bill. "Now tell me a joke."

"Gee—a joke? How come, Trooper Bill?"

"I need a laugh, that's why."

"Oh. Okay. Let me see. Oh yeah, I know a good

joke." Elliot took a long gulp of his drink. "This guy, he goes in to the doctor, because he's not feeling so great. The doctor runs some tests on him. The guy says, 'What's wrong with me, Doc?' 'Bad news,' says the Doc. 'You've got Galactic AIDS, Venusian herpes and Solarian Leprosy.' 'What are you going to do, Doc?' asks the man. 'Well, the first thing I'm going to do is to put you on a diet of pancakes, pizza and tortillas.' 'Why pancakes, pizza and tortillas, Doc?' 'Because they're the only things we'll be able to fit under the door!' "

Bill broke up. He slammed his beer mug on the counter and slapped Elliot on the back. "That's great! That's disgusting! I love it! That's just my kind of Trooper yock!"

"Gee—I'm glad you like it, Bill."

"Now—what say we get some sack-time in before we have to get going."

"Aren't you going to play any of the implant in your ear, Bill?"

"What for? Voluntarily listening to orders without being ordered to? You got a lot to learn. If we have to we'll do it tomorrow morning. What say we round the night off with some more drinks and maybe a look-in at EM's knocking shop if it is open."

"Gee—Bill. That sounds great! What's a knocking shop?"

Yep, thought Bill sinking back into an alcoholic gaze. This guy really was okay. Even if he was incredibly stupid. But there was something about him that bothered Bill . . . like some scampering little lizard, he seemed much too *eager* about the whole thing.

But, *gee*, thought Bill, otherwise this Elliot Methadrine was a good buddy, a nice guy to drink with.

CHAPTER 4

BILL AND ELLIOT FOUND TICKETS WAIT-
ing for them when they arrived at the good ship IC—
Interstellar Cruiser—*Starbloater*. Since Troopers were
only permitted to travel steerage class, Bill was now
sporting a silver set of fake lieutenant's bars that Elliot
had given him. This temporary disguise would last
only for the duration of the trip—but of course it
went instantly to his head. He flared his nostrils, in-
sulted the help, affected a poncey accent and did all
the things that he knew officers did. They were well
on their way in space, Bill enjoying every nonservile
moment of his new existence, when the assassin came
after him with the most terrifying hand blaster that
Bill had ever seen.

A few moments before this happened, Bill was
balanced at the tip of the diving board, dressed in
pink and electric green bathing trunks, holding a can

of beer in his hand and calculating the distance between himself and the pool of opalescent water below him. Bill's muscular midsection was quite red already from the numerous belly flops he'd achieved. He was intent upon making a successful dive this time, even if it killed him.

"What do you think, Elliot? Should I stand back a little bit, or should I balance on the very tip before I go over?"

Elliot watched from his lounge chair intently, taking his time to calculate the equations involved and sipping at an Aldebran Arachne as he did so. "I should think just about where you are will do, Bill. And, gee—maybe you should think about losing the beer can. I think that throws your balance off."

"Yeah," said Bill. He drained the can, crumpled it and tossed it to Elliot. "Good idea. By the way, Elliot. I've been meaning to ask you . . . why do you say 'Gee' all the time?"

That was starting to bother Bill. Not because he had anything against the word "Gee." It was kinda cute, actually. No, what bothered Bill was that Eager Beager at Camp Leon Trotsky had used "Gee" all the time, and he'd turned out to be a Chinger called Bgr who in all of Bill's misadventures had used the word "Gee" quite often. In his guise as Eager Beager, the seven-inch tall creature had utilized a human-looking robot, controlling it from a control booth in the brain-pan.

Bill was becoming suspicious. He'd asked if Elliot wanted to come up for a swim in the ship's pool, figuring that if Elliot sank, then for sure he was a robot. So far, however, Elliot, although he'd donned a very becoming bathing suit, had somehow avoided going for a dip.

Bill and Elliot, following orders from the implant in Bill's left earlobe, had taken berth on the pleasure cruiser IS *Starbloater*, a converted garbage scow reshaped by the Tasteless Plezure Co. to look like an iceberg. ("A cool, COOL cruise," proclaimed the pamphlet.) It was stuffed with officers and their ladies, or girlfriends, or doxies—or boyfriends in many cases—since this was a time for fun. The food was as tasteless as the entertainment, which didn't matter since most of the guests were drunk out of their teeny-tinys most of the time. Getting their kidneys and livers in shape for Barworld. All in all it was pretty revolting; Bill thought it was paradise. Which says more than a bit about his values. Now he waited for an answer to what might be a highly pertinent question.

"Gee, Bill. I don't know. My father and my mother say it all the time. And, after all, I *am* a G-man."

Bill didn't let logic deter him. "You can't think of any other reason?"

"Gee—no. Why does it bother you so much?"

"Well. I knew this Chinger once who said 'Gee' a lot."

"Oh. You mean, Bgr. Yes, we're aware of that. I was wondering when you were going to ask me that question, Bill. But I'm quite happy to answer you. No, I'm not Bgr. Do I look like a seven-foot-tall lizardoid with four arms?"

"Well, no, but—"

"There you go! That problem resolved. Now, as to the problem immediately at hand, why don't you try the implant. It might have an opinion."

As it had turned out, the implant was a marvel of bioelectronics plugged directly into Bill's cerebellum. It had an amazing database of knowledge and some intelligence, and could also be used as a handy pocket calculator. The problem for Bill had been in learning the correct methods of utilizing it without hurting his sore earlobe too much.

Well, Bill rationalized, in this case it was a toss-up between sore ear or even sorer belly.

Bill tugged on his ear. "QUERY: How do I dive in this situation without belly-flopping?"

The device was apparently equipped with all manner of sensor devices hooked to Bill's nervous system—nanochip memory, a rudimentary artificial intelligence, and a nasal voice simulator (funny, thought Bill—a nasal voice in an ear lobe!). What was worse was that the demented programmer who had designed the system also had a love for the ethnic music of long-vanished Earth. He must have tapped a digitized databank from one of the ancient spacers and had dumped it into the RAM in Bill's ear. He had undoubtedly listened to it while working away the weary hours of programming. Fine. But he wrote such crappy software that bits of the music leaked through into the rest of the programs. Something Latin, scratching away at the edge of Bill's hearing, sounded like *Mula Chula*.

"Come on," Bill said, raising his voice to drown out the guitars. "Diving—how do I dive?"

Bill, who'd been expecting trajectory extrapolations and weight/air-resistance/gravity equations, was naturally disappointed.

"*Don't*," he said out loud. "What the bowb do you mean, *don't!* I'm going to get this right if it kills me!"

"Leesten, cabron. You got the grace and reflexes of a grande flamenco dancer—a *dead* grande flamenco dancer!"

"You know, for once I wish you'd be a *machine*

like you're supposed to be and do what I ask," shouted Bill, tugging his ear with exasperation. "And would you stop playing that stupid music and answer the question?"

Elliot Methadrine looked up from the lounge chair. "Gee—talking to your ear again, huh? I wonder why they didn't give that device to me!"

"I certainly wish they had!" Bill twisted the ear hard to shut the stupid thing off. "Now I'm going to dive, and dive right this time, or—"

Bill never got the chance to explain what he would do if he didn't dive right—or belly flop for that matter, although he did end up in the water.

Because that was when the assassin popped out of the service hatch in the deck.

The guy was about five foot nine. He had long shaggy hair and a rainbow-colored headband to keep that hair out of his eyes. He had a goatee and granny glasses. He wore a dirty dyed T-shirt, bell-bottoms, and leather moccasins. From around his neck dangled a large medallion: the peace symbol. In his arms he cradled a Mauser laser cannon: a definite war symbol.

It was the deadliest hand armament Bill had ever seen.

"Die, Imbeerialist Pig!" the guy screeched and pointed the sights and bore of the cannon directly at Bill.

Battle being the line of work he'd chosen (well, not exactly *chosen*, maybe), Bill had had many a gun trained on him. However, since he was now weaponless and in the open, making a fine target, he didn't have many options.

He dove headfirst into the water.

An energy beam fried the air where he'd just been.

Bill hit the water feetfirst and went as deep as he could. He could feel the water boiling above him as the assassin tried to get him through the water. But Bill knew that a sinking target was hard to hit, and there was nothing Bill did in aquatic sports better than sink. Fortunately, he was at the forty-foot-deep end of the pool, so he had a long way to sink. Unfortunately, his lung capacity was not terrific; he had not breathed in deeply before diving, so just as soon as he hit bottom, he had to start thinking about coming up for some air.

Bill was intelligent enough to know that he'd better not come up where he went down. So he swam as far as he could until he banged his head on the side of the pool and then began thrashing back to the surface up the side of the pool, hoping against hope that by the time he'd surface the guy would have been killed by Elliot—and that he wouldn't get the bends.

When he peeped up out of the top of the water, taking a Trooper-sized breath immediately, he saw that the poolside was a total mess. The lounge chair was blown apart, burned towels were everywhere and Elliot's plastic raft and rubber duck lay deflated upon the water. There was the smell of singed flesh in the air.

Bill vaulted out of the pool and ran for cover.

He peeped out from the door marked LADIES.

Someone had been burned, that was for sure . . . but there was no sign of bodies now, charred or otherwise. Bill was about to make a run for the MEN'S room and his clothes when Elliot Methadrine stumbled through the door, walked a few paces and then fell down, moaning. In his right arm he held a small derringer-blaster; his left arm was badly burned.

"Medic!" Bill called out loudly and automatically. "Medic!"

"Gee—maybe the ship's doctor would be a better idea, huh, Bill?" said Elliot Methadrine, grimacing with pain but trying to get up nonetheless. "I doubt if there are any Trooper medics aboard. That guy kind of gave me a good one."

Bill looked down. Nothing good about this wound. One thing good it proved though: no way could this guy possibly be the Chinger called Bgr in a robot suit. This guy was *human*, no question about that.

A human going into shock.

"He sure did do that." Bill went to the phone and called up the ship's emergency medical team. However, it appeared that the emergency forces aboard the STARBLOATER had already been alerted. Red lights started flashing everywhere, and Bill could hear the clatter and thump of running feet. Any moment now help would be on its way.

But before they carted Elliot off, Bill had to ask him something. He had to smack him around a bit to get him back to working consciousness, but finally the guy roused. "Elliot. Who the bowb *was* that guy? And what happened to him?"

"I don't know, Bill," said Elliot. "I winged him, he scorched me, and then alarms started going off and he ran. I chased him down a corridor all the way to the bow. . . . And then he just . . . disappeared."

"You mean, he hid and you couldn't find him. So he's got to be somewhere still on board this ship."

"Gee—No. I mean, *disappeared*. Into thin air. Like a sort of ghost fading out. One moment there he was, wild-eyed and hairy. The next, he just melted into thin air."

"Melted?"

"No, wait. It was like there was this hole. This wavering energy fluctuation . . . and he stepped into it and he was . . . gone."

Elliot took a deep breath. "Gee—Bill. Do you think he's a time traveler? Do you think this is one of the guys we're after . . . and he's trying to get *you* first?"

"I think—" said Bill. "I think that I need a big tumbler of whiskey."

"One more thing, Bill. I recognized him . . . I mean, not personally, but generically. He's a hippie, Bill. A hippie from Hellworld. Do you know what that means, Bill?"

Bill's eyes bugged. "Yeah. That means you need a whiskey too."

CHAPTER 5

A HIPPIE!

From Hellworld!

Bill didn't really know what that meant, but it didn't sound real good. However, Elliot passed out before he could tell him, and was carted off to the ship's sick bay for emergency medical attention. Bill stumbled into the bar and ordered his jug of whiskey—but made sure that he kept a gun, safety off, by his side.

In the dark ship's bar, Bill made discreet inquiries into the exact nature of his would-be assassin.

"Hey, you bowbs," he addressed the assemblage of ancient lieutenants and brain-dead captains, weaving back and forth, red eyes glaring, spittle glistening on his fangs. "Anybody here know what hippies from Hellworld are?"

If anyone knew, they weren't telling. Or were too

wiped out to even hear him. So Bill just ordered a refill and whiled away the time till the arrival of the STARBLOATER at Barworld. Elliot Methadrine was out for a few days. . . . And it never occurred to Bill that his computer earlobe companion might have had the information. . . .

Or maybe he just didn't want to listen to any more ethnic music for a while.

Whatever the case, Bill spent the remainder of the voyage to Barworld prepping his system for what it could expect when they landed.

Booze.

"Gee, Bill! This is a *great* place!" said Elliot Methadrine, gesturing with his good arm. The other one, wrapped in plastiband, hung limply from his shoulder in a cloth sling. The doctors on the STARBLOATER had performed a miracle. In an era of computerized microsurgery, growth replacement and arm-bud implants, they had managed to botch the job totally. Usually, a salvageable arm could be healed up in a few days. However, the doctors had programmed the wrong mixture in the heal-tank and Elliot's arm was going to be out of commission for a while.

"Wow!" agreed Bill enthusiastically. "It sure is something!" He dodged a football that sailed over his head. A group of short-haired, ugly young men in silly-looking armored outfits and helmets began chasing the ball, kicking it and each other. Spectators occasionally got into the action by throwing a punch at one another. All in all there was a terrific spirit of competition and cooperation in the yeasty air.

Bill and Elliot had just docked at Barworld. Following the orders of Bill's ear implant, they had taken a shuttle down to the unusual island of Rosebowl.

Here quaint holograms of old and creakily pictur-
esque buildings leaned in various states of historical
decomposition, modeled on the sprawling skyscrap-
ers and slums of long-vanished Old Earth. Here antique gin joints and cocktail lounges did a roaring
business.

For, after all, this *was* Barworld!

"Gee—how come all the balls, Bill?" Elliot wanted
to know. "The bars I can understand—but what's
with the athletics?"

At a weak, bored moment, back in a bar on the
STARBLOATER, Bill had tugged on his ear, and
got some gloomy Slavic music along with the information he was trying to access.

"Well, you see, Elliot, although Barworld's main
attraction is its bars, it *is* a resort world. It's got a lot
of subdivisions."

"And this one's an island, right?"

"Yeah, that's right. It's a resort for drinking football players and fans."

"What's football?"

"I don't know. I mean I know, I got the explanation, but I couldn't understand a word of it. Something like two yards to conversion of a left out back,
pass the ball and eat the goalpost. Or something like
that."

"Sounds hideously complex. A sport only for intellectuals, I imagine."

"Yeah. The strain of thinking about football ap-
pears to be so great that the fans watch the teams
play and then beat each other up. Once in a while,
just for yucks, they drink themselves senseless, have
a massive stampede and crush hundreds. Great sport,
huh?"

Dodging a wildly hurtling oval ball, Elliot Methadrine said, "Gee—I think I'll stick to potsy, myself."

"What a place, though, huh Elliot?"

"Yeah, Bill," said Elliot sniffing the somewhat sour air uneasily. "Smells like it could use a bar of soap!"

"Ah, you won't notice the smell soon as we sit ourselves down at the place where we're supposed to be going. Uncle Nancy's Cross-Dressing Emporium! We'll have ourselves a couple of drinks and you'll see, we'll get this whole problem solved for the GBI— just like that. And then I'll have something that no other Trooper ever had." A tear of happiness-to-come formed in the corner of his eye, and splashed saltily onto the beer mat. "I'm going to have a furlough, a *vacation!* I still can't believe it, I don't know how to spell it—but I'm going to have one anyway!"

"Sounds good to me, Bill," said Elliot. "I'll take one too. Give this arm a chance to heal."

"Yeah. Sorry about that, Elliot. You know, you saved my life back there. I guess I owe you. Will a drink do?"

"Gee, Bill—I guess maybe you'll be able to save *my* life too before all this is over."

Bill nodded absently, too absorbed in this massive overkill of bars all around him. Some of the boozers had neon signs, while some of them had old-fashioned coats of arms or hanging wooden signs displaying their names and some painted picture. There were bars in all shapes and sizes, bars of all varieties. Unique bars and boutique bars. Small bars, big bars and candy bars. And all of them exuded a sense of community, conviviality, the noise of amiable song or fisticuffs—and the friendly sound of puking. Plus, the multitextured smell of absolutely the best drink that Bill had ever, *ever* encountered.

From orbit, Barworld itself had been quite a sight. The eighth planet from a sun called Billiard III, it appropriately looked like an Eight Ball. Or at least, Bill thought so when he had crawled by mistake onto the observation deck thinking it was the men's room and saw it, nighttime on the planet, against the backdrop of stars as though on Yawah's own pool table. To think! Every sin known to mankind here, with maybe also millions of alien sins to boot—and countries and islands and archipelagos and isthmuses and floating ships and underwater cities filled with bars, bars, bars! The planet of ten thousand bars! This was no accident. The other planets of the Billiard III system, uninhabitable by normal human beings, were vast seas of various kinds of alcoholic beverages. Apparently when this solar system was emerging from the molten to the solid state, the usual complex carbon molecules were formed. However, evolution took a different turn here. There were only plants, no animal life forms at all. This plant life grew and nurtured, absorbing the light from the brilliant sun, making sugar from the volcanic carbon dioxide. And then—oh lucky mutant, valiant sport of nature, cunning spore—the first strain of yeast appeared. Soon the oceans were bubbling with planetwide fermentation. A lovely brew of alcoholic soup came into being. What an ocean!

It would be difficult to explain to a layman the process by which the volcanoes and rock strata combined in a natural form of distillation. But combine they did—and Barworld was born!

Not only that, but parallel evolution on the other planets produced equally exciting results. For example, there was Scotchworld, and Ginworld and Vodkaworld. . . . This freak accident of Nature was viewed as a godsend to the colonists who discovered the only inhabitable world in the system and promptly built bars to service the thirsty travelers of the universe. The Barworlder bosses "mined" the other planets by using genetically altered alien beings suited to the various atmospheres. They used these siphoned libations in the taverns of Barworld, or shipped them away as export products to other star systems. The label—a planet with a tap—on Barworld products had become famous galaxywide for quality. It was also prohibitively expensive, and Bill had only actually had a taste of Barworld's version of imitation Dingleberry wine . . . but it had tasted great!

And now, he was here!

Utilizing a map downloaded from his earlobe memory bank, Bill and Elliot traveled along the streets, looking for their destination, avoiding crazed sportsmen and their wildly careening balls. Bill got distracted by an advertising flyer promising scantily clad blondes and vats of champagne, but Elliot suggested he save it for later, when he'd have more time. Finally, they found the place right where the map said it would be—once the mustard stain was removed.

"This is it!" said Bill excitedly, pointing up at the old-fashioned sign dangling from a post by two chains. "Uncle Nancy's."

Elliot looked up at it uncertainly, scratching his head. "What's that on the sign?"

"Looks like a short-haired woman in a long dress," said Bill, not really interested. What Bill was interested in was wrapping both hands around one of the famous Barworld gallon-sized drinking glasses rumored to be used in such taverns. First some beer

swilled and savored, then they could think about finding this Time Nexus and the Chingers and whatever
the hell they were supposed to be doing. The important stuff, though, was the fabled *dark* stuff. Bill
smacked his lips. The very thought made his salivary
glands work overtime. His fangs were glistening and
dripping.

"Gee—no, Bill, I don't think that's what's on the
sign. Actually, it looks like a *man* wearing a dress!"

"Can't be," Bill said with moronic simplicity.
"Men don't wear dresses." He nodded to himself
with alcoholic satisfaction at his wit.

There was an anteroom before the main bar, and
a man's head poked out of what seemed to be a cloakroom. The cheerful sounds of masculine drinking and
singing and swearing wafted through the old-
fashioned oaken doors.

Beside himself with excitement, Bill grabbed hold
of a door handle.

"Hey, bub," growled a bass voice from the cloak
room. "Where da hell do ya thinks youse guys are
goin', dressed like that?"

"Gee," said Elliot brightly. "Why, we're going
into the bar and have a nice cold beer!"

"We got money!" said Bill, already tasting the future. "Don't worry."

"Dat's okay, bub. I knows ya do. But cha can't go
in there with dose duds on. 'Gainst house dress rules.
C'mere, and maybe I can help you out."

As Bill's eyes adjusted to the dim light, he was
astounded to see that the guy leaning over the top of
the half-door—a beefy bozo with crewcut hair and a
cigar sticking out of the side of a scarred and ugly
face any Trooper DI would be proud to wear (and
usually did)—was wearing a low-cut magenta chiffon

ballroom dress, dark thick chest hair spilling indelicately over the bodice.

"Pretty nice, huh?" said the man proudly, seeing that Bill was ogling his threads. "I got it on sale at Bloomers!"

"Gee—yeah!" said Elliot. "Real nice! But what's wrong with what we've got on now?"

"Nothin'. You just ain't wearing it inside Uncle Nancy's. You want to drink at Uncle Nancy's Cross-Dressing Emporium, you gotta wear a nice dress. House rules. Love it or shove it. Youse got a problem with that?"

Bill was aghast. "No way am I going to put on a woman's dress! Not for nothing or for nobody!"

But then, even as he spoke, the seductive smell of brewed hops wafted through the door cracks.

"Actually, Bill, it's really rather becoming. Quite fetching in fact."

"Shut up," Bill suggested.

"No, really and truly. You look good in green. And the material's clearly top quality, and I like the cut. Maybe the Troopers should think about using ballroom frocks for formal occasions."

"What, like formal latrine cleaning? Formal KP? I'm beginning not to like this."

Bill was feeling quite uncomfortable. He'd practically lived in his Trooper jumpsuit, sleeping in it, even taking baths in it. Now that he was out of it and into the long green dinner dress, he felt strange. It was strange having turgid bar air moving up his hairy legs, to his Trooper BVDs. He felt positively naked. Thank heavens the joker in the cloakroom had let them keep their weapons. ("No problem with the guns, buster. Man's gotta have his gun. But your pants gotta stay here with me.'')

Elliot wore a cute silver lamé costume with a plunging neckline and no back, with a broad black belt and black pumps to match. Elliot was all smiles, seeming to actually be enjoying himself, though he did seem to have a little trouble navigating in the pumps. Bill was just grateful the guy with the cigar let him keep his Trooper boots (''Just as long as the dress is floor-length, Mack, we don't care what kind of canal boats you got on your feet.'')

Uncle Nancy's Cross-Dressing Bar itself was everything that Bill dreamed it would be. It was all wood and decorated mirrors, with paintings of nude women on the walls. Low lights. A fireplace. Well-padded furniture. Nice red rug. And the bar stretched forever, a gorgeous mahogany wonder with sleek feminine lines, polished to a high gloss. The back shelves were packed with bottles of spirits. And there was a bewildering array of taps, all differently shaped and colored: beer and ale, pulque and cider! All clothed in the soft alcoholic glow, the scent of many pleasantly imbibed brews and briefly bolted shots.

In short, it was Bill's idea of heaven.

The strange thing, of course, was that it was filled with men wearing dresses. Culottes and miniskirts and long flowing dresses. Different colors and shapes and sizes of dresses from different historical eras. The men in the dresses, despite how odd they looked, behaved much as men in lumberjack outfits or military outfits or civilian outfits might. They were talking and laughing and slapping each other on the back, all in good macho spirit and convivial ranges of drunkenness as they downed their drinks. For Bill, though, it was awfully difficult to ignore the fact that they all wore dresses. It was even more difficult for

Bill to ignore the fact that *he* wore a dress.

A couple of empty bar stools sang their siren song. Bill gestured toward them. "Glrrk. I really need a drink now."

"Gee, sure Bill!" said Elliot. "On me!"

They sat by a guy in a nice gingham getup, who said nothing.

"Now, run this by me again, Bill," said Elliot. "*This* is supposed to be the place where the Time Distortion Nexus is?"

"That's right," said Bill. "I'll consult the computer AI again on the details. And we'll figure what we have to do then. But right now, mind if we just have a few drinks, shoot the breeze with the locals and get the lay of the land, so to speak?"

"Gee—sure Bill. I do confess that I could use a bit of a libation myself. That shuttle down was a little hard even for a guy who's used to Gs!"

They settled down onto the comfortable stools and leaned against the bar. Bill savored the glossy texture of the bar. Yes, a guy could get lost here. Especially with the aid of one of these tankards of drink. For sure enough, all of the men were drinking out of Brobdignagian beer steins, their faces and noses pleasantly coated with beer foam.

Eagerly, Bill held up a finger for service.

A bartender instantly appeared to take their order. "And how can I be of service to you gentlemen?"

Bill opened his mouth to order, but nothing came out. He realized that he was so excited about getting a drink of genuine Barworld booze that he was absolutely flummoxed about what brand to order first. There were absolutely so many to choose from.

"Ahh . . . Ahhh . . . Ahhhh . . ."

The bartender was round-face, red-nosed, round-bellied as well—with a beard and tresses and a beautiful red dress with flounces. His entire aspect gleamed with conviviality. "Ah yes. A first-timer. This happens often." He turned to Elliot. "I assume this is your friend's first time on Barworld."

"How did you know?" said Elliot.

"First-Timer's Syndrome. Common problem. Now then, what do you think your friend would like—and by the way, those dresses you're wearing look absolutely *smashing*." The bartender cast a glance back at the panoply of available potables. "Hmmm. What have we got here? How about some nice wine, straight from the vats of Vinworld, newly stomped by Feet Critters and then fermented in Uncle Nancy's own special casks?"

"Ergghh," said Bill, shaking his head *no* adamantly. "Ergghhh!"

"Ah! Perhaps some of our spirits! We've a very nice price on Bourbon today, so smoothly sweet that it bring tears of pure pleasure!"

"Gee—no," said Elliot. "I think what my friend and I would really like are two of those mammoth glasses of draught beer... But you have so many brands!"

Bill nodded his head up and down, gasping. Almost choking on his own anticipatory saliva.

"Oh dear, your friend has Drool Syndrome. A common phenomenon for *all* of us thirsty folk here on Barworld. Beer, then. Not ale, not cider..." The man glanced speculatively along the row of dozens of possibilities. "Bitter would you like? Or perhaps some cold lager."

"I guess Bill would like something that tastes good.

Working for the Emperor, we don't get much of that."

"Ah! I know! Today's Second Best Bitter! Strange Old Blackheart!" The barkeep grabbed a couple of the huge glasses.

"Er—Second Best? Why not the Best?"

"Because, sadly, Old *Very* Strange and Peculiar is all sold out, I'm afraid. But really, they're all excellent. Best Bitter is just a term hereabouts." He'd already started a tap, and dark foamy stuff was pouring out of spigots like nobody's business, quickly filling up the gallon glass. He started topping up the other one. "I'm sure this will hit your friend's spot." He hefted the large glass in front of Bill.

Bill picked it up and drank. He drank and drank and drank, and when he had to pause for breath, only a small portion of the liquid was gone! He drank some more and then had to put the glass down and give himself a break from so much incredible pleasure.

Gustatory orgasm!

Oh sheaves of hops and wheat, pure tasty water, artificially blended and formulaically fermented to tickle the taste buds! Bill experienced waves of wistful visions, a warmth flowing through him like the kiss of an ever faithful lover. Ah, sublime bliss. This was the very breath of tasty poetry!

Bill wiped his mouth on his sleeve and belched daintily.

"Yow! That's *incredible!*" he gasped.

"And so we observe the Satisfaction Syndrome," said the barkeep, putting Elliot's glass in front of him. Elliot tasted the stuff and agreed that it was truly wonderful.

Bill's next impulse was to drink more, but something stopped him. After his eruction was satisfactorily completed, he was in such a convivial mood, he felt like communing with his fellow man! "I'm Bill. With two Ls. And this is my partner, Elliot! We're tourists!"

"Gee—that's right. Tourists!" said Elliot.

"Well, glad to meet you, Bill and Elliot!" said the barkeep. "I'm Uncle Nancy."

"Uncle Nancy. Gee—the owner?"

"That's right," said Uncle Nancy, obviously pleased with himself. "None other."

"So tell me, Uncle Nancy. Give me the scoop, huh?" Bill looked around, grinning, at the crowd. "How come all the men here have to wear dresses?"

"You'll understand fully when you're dead drunk and in a dress, Bill!" said Uncle Nancy, grinning. "Now then, maybe I'd better see to some other customers!"

"Gee—excuse me, Mr. Uncle Nancy," said Elliot. "But aren't those *books* along those shelves up there?" He was looking up and Bill followed his gaze. Sure enough, in the dark recesses of the overhanging ceiling, a long row of books hung. Alongside this was a placard with a Latin inscription:

Veni, bibi, transvestivi.

"They certainly are!" said Uncle Nancy, his grin getting broader.

"What's the Latin inscription?" asked Elliot.

"'I came, I drank, I dressed cross-sex!'" replied Uncle Nancy.

"Gee, Mr. Uncle Nancy," said Elliot. "All these books . . . are you a Commupop?"

Suddenly the roar of conversation died to total silence. All heads swiveled Elliot's way. Jaws tensed. Muscles bulked. Knuckle sandwiches were formed.

"Hell no!" said Uncle Nancy. "But that doesn't mean that a virile man can't *read*, does it?"

"Gee—it depends—" Elliot started. But Bill clamped his hand over his mouth.

"What my friend means to say is that he's happy to see that you've got so many terrific-looking books."

The tension broken, people went back to their conversation.

Bill breathed an inward sigh of relief. He personally had nothing against books. He just preferred comix, that was all. He had always been a live-and-let-live kind of guy, this attitude forced upon him by the imperative logic that he liked to live as well. So he personally had nothing against works of literature. And, anyway, he never did learn to read very well. No college degrees down on the farm! Forget books—he was on Barworld! Bring on the Chingers!

"Yeah—glad you like 'em!" said Uncle Nancy. He pointed to another large shelf of leather-bound books above the liquor bottles running the full length of the bar. "That's my personal collection of the classics. Let me show you how nicely put together these rare volumes are. Some of them are said to date back to Earth itself. Which of course can't be possible but is nice to think about."

With great reverence and care he selected one of the books and placed it before Bill and Elliot. Soft vellum. Gilt edged. Black and red. A thing of beauty indeed. Even Bill was impressed.

"DAVID COPPERFIELD, by Charles Dickens," Bill read. "Is that about mining?"

"No! It's one of the classics, Bill!" said Uncle Nancy. "A wonderful book about a coming of age in the early Victorian era."

"It stinks!" said a surly, whiny voice behind Bill. "It's a piece of garbage." Bill looked around and was startled to see behind him the hippie from Hellworld who had tried to fry him!

CHAPTER 6

NO, IT WASN'T.

Actually, the guy just *looked* like the hippie from Hellworld who had taken a shot at Bill and had incinerated Elliot's arm. Although he wore the same long hair, headband, and bell bottoms, he was a good deal taller and huskier, pimplier and grayer.

And of course, over all this, the repulsive joker was wearing a dress—a very unattractive flower-print muu-muu, actually.

"It sucks," said the man adamantly. There was a wild gleam of anarchy in his eye.

"I thought I told you hippies I didn't want to see you around my place," said Uncle Nancy.

"Gee—I don't know, it sure looks like a real good book," Elliot ameliorated. "What kind of books do you prefer?"

The guy ground his teeth and snorted. He smelled

of Kona gold and psychedelic tea. His breath, other than possessing a case of terminal halitosis, was redolent with macroantibiotic food. "I like . . ." he said the words with a fierce defiance. "Horny-Porny!"

"Well, yeah," said Bill, taking an agreeable swig of beer. "I like horn-po too!"

Without warning, the guy grabbed Bill by the front of his dress. "Don't call it that, man! It's not ho-po or horn-poo or any of those prole acronyms, hear? It's just good old down country horny-porny!"

"Gee, Mister!" said Elliot. "No need to take offense!"

Normally, Bill would have just belted the guy and started up a nice, proper barroom brawl. However, Bill felt uncomfortable with the idea of fighting in a dress—it wasn't ladylike. And the dress might get torn. "Sorry, old buddy. Didn't mean nothing. Buy you a drink?"

The guy looked nervous. "Yeah. I guess maybe I could use a stiff drink."

"A stiff's drink—that's like formaldehyde, right?" barked Uncle Nancy sarcastically. "I think that's a good idea, bud. Too bad I only have good liquor here."

Bill, who had indeed imbibed formaldehyde before and seriously felt that even the dead shouldn't have to take it, shook his head. "Ah, Uncle Nancy. Let's keep things pleasant here." He was relaxing into a glowing alcoholic stupor and wanted everyone to enjoy it. "I'm having a good time, let's all have a good time. Why don't you just give my hairy friend here the most alcoholic brew you got on tap or inna bottle!"

"Comin' up in a jiffy!" The bartender pulled open a drawer, and pulled up a small bottle with a red wrapper. On the wrapper were the words, in Olde English Calligraphy, *Olde Mortality*, and in very small print *Ye be informed no person hath ever lived to finish ye whole bottle*.

"I want one too," Bill intoned with alcoholic greed.

"Me three," Elliot said in the same voice.

"Last one," Uncle Nancy told them. "But I got three bottles of fermented yak's milk I will gladly share with you. A favorite tipple of mine this time of day." He quickly opened the bottles, seized one by the neck and passed the others over. "Here's to a good yak," he said, almost draining his.

The drink tasted like nothing Bill had experienced before, settling to the pit of his stomach and exploding there. But good!

Bill's eyes watered with joy. He tried to express his joy, but when he tried to speak all he could say was "Mooo!"

"Yep," said Uncle Nancy, wiping away tears of his own. "This stuff is the real stuff—Moo!"

Elliot Methadrine could only sip his. But the hippie sneered at this abstemiousness and drained his own drink all the way down in a single gulp. Plumes of steam seemed to rise from his ears. But instead of being more relaxed—or dead—the guy's eyes just looked a little wilder. Apparently, not for the first time, the commercial had lied.

"So anyway," said Uncle Nancy, folding his arms together on his chest with disapproval. "What exactly brings a thing like you into my joint?"

"Hey, man, don't rag me," muttered the hippie. "I'm tryin' to remember. I'm *so* spaced out, man. Must have been something I smoked. Or drank. Or shot up. Or something."

Bill drained his bottle and banged his empty pint down onto the counter. "Better fill me up with regular. Draft. Lasts a little longer." Bill was feeling positively buoyant. Usually alcohol hammered closed the lid on the loose stuff slogging around in his head. This dark, delicious stuff was actually exhilarating him.

"Gee," said Elliot. "None of that sounds very good."

"It ain't man, it ain't. I think I downed, like, a *blotter* of *acid*, man."

"That must have burned."

"Not too bad," said Bill. "Can bè tasty if properly diluted. Still, I'll never be able to *touch* it now. This stuff is *spoiling* me."

A big frown wrapped around Uncle Nancy's face. "I think the guy's talking about the lysergic dyethelamine variety."

"Huh?"

"A psychotropic substance that alters one's perception of reality," said Elliot, hazarding another sip of his potent drink.

"Hmmm. Sounds interesting," said Bill. "What proof is it?"

"Oh, man. This dude is *bumming* me *out!*" said the hippie. His eyes seemed to bug from his head, as though pulsing with angst from within. "Man . . . those books up there . . . they're *bumming* me out too. No good, no good."

Uncle Nancy snarled in annoyance and, fed up, was reaching under the bar for his leather-bound club when the hippie suddenly stood up straight, raising his hands up into the air with an attitude reeking of 'Eureka!'

"I remember! I remember now! I remember what

I'm supposed to do here!" he cried joyfully.

"What?" said Uncle Nancy, still clutching the club.
"Pray tell, what's that?"

"Gimme a shot of Old Overcoat!"

Clearly unnerved by the man's fierce insistence,
Uncle Nancy obeyed, pouring the amber stuff into
a double shot glass. The wild-eyed man belted it back
with an enthusiasm truly unbridled. He reached over
the bar, grabbed the bartender by bodice and bra and
pulled him toward him. The club was torn from Uncle Nancy's grasp before he could use it.

"You got a little boy's room, man? I gotta go!"

Stunned, Uncle Nancy pointed to the rear of the
establishment. Before anyone could do anything, the
hippie grabbed the almost-full bottle of Old Overcoat
and bolted for the toilet like a man truly obsessed.

"Geronimo!" he cried.

And he was gone.

"Don't know why," said Uncle Nancy. "But I got
a really bad feeling about that guy!"

"Gee—" Elliot supplicated. "So do I."

Bill spilled and dribbled beer with happy incontin-
ence. "Sounds like that guy had a good idea," he
muttered. He took another long sip of his beer. He
happily let the alcoholic stuff run down his throat,
gurgling like an unfettered stream of Bacchus. He
knew now that when he died, he wanted to die choking to death on this wonderful brew.

When he brought his smacking lips away from the
rim of the mug, he noticed that things seemed . . .
well, mighty *different*.

At first, Bill ascribed the difference to a state of
extreme inebriation on his part. But then he realized
that usually when things got this strange, he was
usually flat on his face staring at the floor. Now,

however, he was sitting in a perfectly upright position, if not sober then fully in control of his capacities.

The whole bar had changed.

Gone was the dusky, comfortable wood, the dark, smoky mood. In its place were bright lights, the sheen of metal, plastic and glass, the flash of mirrors. The air smelled not of beer and chintz and tobacco, but of sweat and talc and spandex.

Bill blinked at how bright it was. His astonishment turned to alarm. In any situation of panic, and if there is alcohol close by, a good Trooper knows what to do. Finish your drink.

Bill grabbed the glass in front of him and drank liberally of its contents...

And spit it out, gasping.

It was some strange combination of fruit and yogurt and the Devil knew what else. Bill had heard of this kind of nonalcoholic and disgusting libation before—but he'd never let it close to his lips.

He wiped his mouth free of it on a sleeve. He'd just drunk (gasp!) a *health* shake!

What had happened to his beer?

He looked to Uncle Nancy for explanation, and was startled to see that the bartender no longer wore a dress. Rather, he was wearing a dark blue sweat suit, open at the neck to let part of his plethora of salt-and-pepper chest hair out. Bill looked down and saw that *he* was no longer wearing a dress, nor was Elliot Methadrine. They both sported bright green and red gym shorts and T-shirts.

Grunts brought Bill's attention over to the far side of the room, where mammothly muscled males were in the process of lifting weights.

"This isn't Barworld anymore," said Elliot, without a shred of his previous tentativeness. "It's turned to Barbellworld!"

"My dress!" a man cried. And another plaint: "What happened to my lovely dress!"

"The hippie!" said Elliot, snapping his fingers. He pointed toward the Men's Room. "That bathroom wouldn't happen to be the location of the Time/Space Resonation Nexus?"

Uncle Nancy blinked. "Well, yeah, maybe—I mean, all the bars use Time/Space Plumbing system—I don't know about no nexus."

"That's it, Bill! That must be it!" Elliot intoned loudly. He pulled off his bright purple bandana and threw it onto the floor in disgust. "What we were looking for was right under our noses, and we didn't even notice. You were so insistent upon getting your stupid booze!"

"What's wrong with that?" Bill whined defensively. "It *is* Barworld. Or it was, anyway." He cast a doubtful and blurry eye toward the men working out with weights. On the far wall were posters depicting Mr. Planetary and Mr. Nebula and Mr. Lightspeed, flexing muscles like mutated melons.

"My books!" cried Uncle Nancy.

"What—are they gone?"

"No—but look, they've . . . they've *changed.*"

Bill looked down. Sure enough, they had changed. At first he didn't see it, but when he looked more closely, he saw exactly how they had altered.

What had once been DAVID COPPERFIELD by Charles Dickens was now PECS GALORE by I. Liftem, while WAR AND PEACE by Leo Tolstoy had become BICEPS AND TRICEPS by Bod Builder.

"My books. My great literature!" cried Uncle Nancy, even more disturbed over this than the loss of his dress. "It's all been changed into muscled moron crapola!"

"I smell a time-changer at work!" intoned Elliot Methadrine. "Definitely the work of that crazed hippie who just left—but how did he do it? I haven't got the faintest idea."

Bill didn't have the faintest idea, either. He was too busy undergoing, first, shock, then the distinct beginnings of an anxiety attack. Imagine—a lifelong search for the Fountain of Youth (well, the Fountain of Vermouth, anyway) only to have that luscious flow yanked untimely from one's mouth. Horrors! He'd found Barworld and yet all that there was to drink was—he shuddered at the thought—*health shakes?*

"What . . . What could that bowbhead hippie possibly have done?" he queried incoherently, his jaw flapping like a bar door in the wind.

"I'll tell you what he did!" Elliot intoned grotesquely. "I mean, really, are you that dense? He's gone back to the past and changed history."

Uncle Nancy looked despairingly at his books, tearing out handfuls of hair from his rapidly balding head.

"Does this mean—we've failed?" Bill mumbled, losing track of things.

"I don't know. Let's find out." Elliot strode over to a hunk manfully gulping Evian water, dabbing at a sweating forehead between sets. "A question, sir. Is there still a war going on with the Chingers?"

"Chingers," said the man with a definite Austrian accent. "Oh! Ja, ja. I remember them from my school lessons. Ja! Dey vere *viped* out like the wermin dey vere. A hundert years ago!"

"Well," said Bill, "that's good news anyway."

"Ja, unt dat vas by der Fourth Reich, too. Sieg heil!" said the Austrian, saluting a picture of a man with a very tiny mustache on the wall. "Der Glorious Fourth Reich, who also abolished alcohol unt tobacco. Und put der barbell on the map of history."

"No more alcohol!" wailed Bill, dumbstruck. His personal universe had just ended.

"This calls for radical action," said Elliot. He pulled out an ID badge. "My name is Elliot Methadrine and I'm with the Interdimensional Time Crime Enforcement."

"The Time Cops!" said Uncle Nancy, clearly impressed. "Hey, you guys used to stop in all the time for free drinks and bribes.

"I thought you were with the GBI," said Bill.

"No need for that cover now, Bill," said Elliot, suddenly all business. "I was following a lead but it has just gone south. Too late to stop it now." He turned back to the bodybuilder. "I need to requisition street clothing and weapons."

"Ja. Sure," said the muscle-bound fellow. "Vee got dat real love for der Police. Vee respect der Authority on Barbellworld. It vas der vish of our founder, St. Arnold, that ve be good, clean, reverent, sadistic muscle pumpers!"

"Fine, fine," said Elliot. "Uncle Nancy—how does the Time/Space Plumbing work? Clearly the hairy guy did something in there. Where are the guts, the *controls* to the thing?"

"Well, hell if I know," said Uncle Nancy, his big beefy face growing red. "I'm not a Time Sanitation Plumber. We use Chronos Sewage ourselves, and they take forever to get out here. We'll just have to go take a look, won't we?"

"Come on, Bill," said Elliot Methadrine. "Let's get a change of clothes and then go have a look."

Bill grimaced and shook his head woefully.

Talk about things going down the tubes!

CHAPTER 7

UNCLE NANCY SHOWED BILL AND ELLIOT to the bathroom.

"Revolting! Just look how this thing has changed!" groused the bartender, gazing around in horror at the colorful tile, the new light fixtures, the bidets, the vitamin and cologne vending machines. "Used to be just a trough and a thundermug. Oh yeah—and a rubber dispenser that was always broken or empty. Real homey and friendly with lots of grafitti. And I mean graphic grafitti."

Bill, a little woozy, looked at the three bright white porcelain urinals. "Gotta go," he mumbled.

"Not there, you idiot!" said Elliot. "Didn't you hear the man? That's the Time Vortex!"

Bill blinked. Funny, looked like a urinal to him. True, an unusually fancy, unusually clean urinal. "Sorry—I guess I can wait. . . ."

The bartender and Bill stared, transfixed, as Elliot reached out a tremulous hand, touched the handle on the urinal, sucked in a deep breath—and flushed.

The results were far more dramatic than usual. It even beat the cheap vacuum potties on quickly assembled starships where chances were you finished your trip with a high squeaky voice.

"Wow!" Bill sussurated.

"Absolutely," Elliot agreed. From somewhere, a small device with knobs and switches and an oscilloscope had appeared in his hands. "According to my Time Ticker—all we Time Police are equipped with these things—what we have here is a crack in Time far larger than anticipated. Yes—I can see how it was possible for that weirdo hippie to jump back through time and wreak havoc. This aperture you could fit an elephant through!"

Bill stepped back two paces and grabbed hold of the door latch of the bathroom stall for security. He felt like he was losing his sense of balance. He had the distinct sensation of being sucked into a mammoth Time Maw.

The Portal had replaced the porcelain facility completely. A scintillating light swirled and revolved and gave off sparks, whirling and growing. Dimly seen within this display was a control console, not unlike a multidialed TV set. As the Time-Wind pulsed, the screen flickered and displayed some highly interesting scenes.

Bill sniffed loudly. "It stinks," he said nasally, because he was pinching his nostrils shut as he spoke.

"Of course. That is because the Time-Nexus is routed through Garbageworld on its way to linkup to Barworld. Depends on what part of the past you tune into," said Elliot. "This particular era, for instance, is particularly offensive to members of our era." He tapped his nose. "Which is why Time Authority knocks out its agents' sense of smell before we Time Dump."

"And just what era would that be? That you're from I mean," Uncle Nancy wanted to know.

"Classified information," stated Elliot unequivocally. Hair waving, he looked down at his device. Its needles were swinging wildly. A hot red light flashed. And the oscilloscope was being particularly scilly. "Yikes!" intoned Elliot, looking alarmed and rather uncharacteristically out of control. "This time portal—"

"Don't tell me," cried Uncle Nancy. "Something terrible is going to happen and we'll all be killed!"

"No. Well, possibly maybe yes. Anything could happen—because this thing, this Time Portal, and I find this difficult to comprehend, is sentient!"

"That's kind of a long word," Bill explained. "It means, I guess—sentiment without the 'M' because it's not quite as emotional?"

"No, moron. It means alive! Alive and intelligent! Which is more than I can say for you sometimes!" Elliot Methadrine shook his head with alarm and amazement. "In all my eras as a Time Agent, I've never seen such a thing!"

"Alas, I encounter your deplorable type all too often," a rich baritone bass said. British accent, deep-dipped with culture, heavily dripping irony and other metallic forms of humor. "Good day, you wretched deplorable exuses for biological self-propagation. In the words of my esteemed ancestors, Alexander Graham Time-Phone Machine, you rang?"

The Time Portal glowed ethereally, a fascinating sight. Its interior was imbedded with alien crystalline assemblages and jewellike appendages emanating rainbowed glow and pixillating auras, light arias and perhaps even light operas, Haydn perhaps, or Delius—or was that THE MIKADO by Gilbert and Sullivan in the background? Upon those aforementioned screens flashed candid scenes from intergalactic history. The signing of the Declaration of Independence. The Emperor's Annual Public Constitutional. Napoleon the Fifth's Battle of Watercloset.

"You . . . You're a Time Portal?" intimated Bill, gasping gawkily with awe.

"Well, I'm certainly not a Time Potable, so please refrain from drinking me, you obvious lush! Nor am I a Time Portable. I am the full-scale, full-priced model—an Eton- and Oxford-educated Time Portal. And dear chap it is a pitiable shame that as worthy an intelligence as I am, I must respond to anyone who yanks my chain, so to speak. Especially noisome and illiterate obnoxious primates such as yourself."

"Well, be that as it may," intoned Elliot, rearing up to his full if meager height. "As you have just told us, in far too much detail, you have been summoned and you must help us!" Elliot flashed his Time Cop identification and then showed the Portal his Captain Cosmic Secret Decoder ring.

"Yeah, right!" said Uncle Nancy. "And first off we want to know where the hell did that hairy guy who zipped in here get to?"

"What's that, dear boy? Hirsute chappy, you say? Ah! Of course! You must mean that horrible hippie from Hellworld. Yes, quite! Why, I believe he went back into the past, and with the rather laudable ambition to change history. Either that or I plugged a few too many bloody nanodes into my quazoid last night."

"Just take a look," said Bill. "He must have changed something. This dump used to be a nice dump of a bar! Now it's a sweaty gym, run by goosestepping weightlifters with German accents."

"Hmm. Oh, my, yes. Well, that sort of thing does happen occasionally. You can't have Time Portals in this Universe and not get a few minor changes from time to time."

"Minor changes!" expostulated Elliot Methadrine. "We're talking about a vast sweeping cataclysm! Why, I'm not even sure there's a Galactic Bureau of Investigation anymore!"

An amber light pulsed quizzically. "Oh?" said the Time Portal. "Well, then. Let's have a look into my Crystal Bowl." From the bottom of the Portal's floor emerged a round bowl filled with scintillating liquid. In this liquid swam a goldfish. Pictures began to flash. Bill saw images of Panzer-tanks and Spandau propeller planes. Jackboots kicking galactic butt. Beer halls and pretzels everywhere. Hmm, he thought. Maybe this change isn't really bad. He loved beer halls and pretzels!

Finally, the flipping images settled upon a wobbling close-up of a sign. "There you go, lads!" said the Portal. "Images of the Way Things Are Now. 'GALACTIC BUREAU OF INVESTIGATION,'" he read. "You see, things haven't changed so much! One totalitarian government is much the same as another. I say, amongst all those amino acids and yogurt drinks out there at that refreshment station, I don't suppose you might find me a spot of tea and maybe a lightly toasted crumpet or two?"

Bill squinted at the sign. "It's a sign for a ship!" he exclaimed with some satisfaction at his astute powers of observation—although in truth he could read it better because he had a superior angle to the others.

"A ship?" said Uncle Nancy.

"Yes! See . . . off to the side . . . it says 'SS GAL-ACTIC BUREAU OF INVESTIGATION.'"

"Good grief, Bill!" said Elliot. "That's not a ship! That's the SS! The infamous secret police of the Nazi party!"

Bill blinked. "Yeah. Well, what's the difference? Aren't you guys the infamous secret police who blackmail any politician who is at least one percent honest and always steal the spiked punch at the Emperor's party?"

"So they're the rotten bastards!" said Uncle Nancy. "I always wondered about that!"

Elliot Methadrine screwed his face up and pounded on the side of his head with his fists in total frustration. "Look, Time Portal! In the name of Truth, Order, Justice and Equilibrium in the Universe—"

"You got some Librium?" interrupted Bill. "I sure could use some."

"Shut up, Bill!" Elliot suggested to the Trooper as he ground his teeth gratingly, then turned back to the Portal. "You have to help us avert this . . . this chaos. You must take us back to the place in time where that hippie went to change the course of history. What he has done is terrible! Where was it?"

"Hmm? The Time that hirsute individual went? Why, I declare! It is rather boring, but demn me, I am driven to admit that it has completely slipped my memory. I suppose I could have a crafty riffle through my files and come up with the information. Though—do pardon my yawn—I must admit I'm not terribly motivated."

"Oh . . . and dare I ask just what motivated you to acquiesce to the hippie's demands?"

The light auras formed a quiescent Technicolor Cheshire cat grin. "Since we are being frank, dear boy—hard cold cash, actually."

Elliot slapped his forehead with exasperation. "Just who the hell are you anyway, guy?" He took out a pen and a small spiral notebook. "I want your name, your serial number, your registration code with Intergalactic Time Machines!"

"Utter rubbish!" boomed the voice insouciantly. "Not applicable. For I am a member of an incredibly ancient, unregistered race of Time Portals. My name is Dudley D. Doo, Esquire, of the Noble Right Royal Transubstantiated Knights of the Temporal Jet Plane. My kind has been around since Before Time Began— and even earlier!"

"Before Time Began?" muttered Bill, trying to imagine that concept. But his mind, such as it was, got even more bent than usual in the process. "You mean, like before they had clocks and digital watches and stuff?" His brain suddenly grasped an important macroscientific concept. "You mean, back when bars never closed!"

"Precisely, chum. And what jolly days they were," said Dudley. "But then, come to think of it, they weren't days, were they? Days hadn't been invented yet. Nor nights. It was just one continual spifflicated party, with time out for an occasional brawl or bash at the birds. Raucous and tiring—but what jolly fun!"

"Breathtaking!" breathed Bill, his eyes wandering off, his mind permanently bent now at the very notion.

"The Knights Temporal!" said Elliot, voice hushed now with awe. "There were rumors of you back at headquarters—and phone numbers in the loo, too! Why, we've found ruins of an ancient civilization from beyond recorded posterity! Could those have belonged . . . to your kind?"

"Not really. I believe that it is a matter of public record that the Knights Temporal are from beyond recorded posteriors!" answered Dudley in a thoroughly smug fashion.

"Hmmm. Guess that makes you guys the butts of jokes!" snorted Uncle Nancy the Bartender.

"Access to the Knights Temporal is one of the Fundamental Keys to the Universe, and a hell of a cheap way to travel!" said Elliot. "However could the hippies from Hellworld have obtained that kind of access?"

Uncle Nancy scratched his head. "Robbed banks?"

"No. No!" Elliot paced the floor. "This is far too crucial, too fundamental an issue! We don't know enough about these hippies, dammit! But I can't help but feel as though an understanding of their access to the Knights Temporal—and a comprehension of you knights yourselves—is crucial to the success of this mission!"

The shining Portal glowed a positively numinous sheen with pleasure at the prospect of explaining the story of the Knights Temporal.

"Ahem!" he began. "In the beginning, even before Marmite and traffic wardens, Certificates of Deposit and talkie movies, there was a good deal of nothing but space and absolutely no time for anything or anybody. The local cosmic galactic race at that time first invented overdraughts and Irish jokes to try to make sense of things. That's our lot, mind you—the Knights Temporal. However, needless to say, none of this really worked, since often as not you finished doing something before you began, which caused all manner of confusion and made it rather difficult to calculate interest on CDs. 'What we need,' posited a singularly intelligent gentleman Knight Philospher-Scientist, Simon Temporal, 'is some sort of order to this wretched chaos. I mean, when you don't know when it is the right hour of the day to take tea, that's not civilization.'

"And so Simon Temporal invented the idea of Time. This startling and revolutionary concept was such a profound notion that at first it was far too cosmic an idea for general dissemination and it took a few eons to assimilate. But when it did, the suns and planets started to tick off those days and years like wretched cosmic clockwork, erstwhile life ebbed and flowed, civilizations flowered and died. Although the ultimate boring truth at the core of it all was that it all has about as much relevance as a monkey's ballocks in a nunnery, at least you could measure how many years of boring nothingness an average life held.

"Now this was all very well and now we could soft-boil eggs just right, but for the Knights Temporal, you understand, it was all just a concept. You see, time is actually just a kind of brainwashing on a gross atomic level. It really doesn't exist for us, unless we imagine it does, utilizing these stainless steel and crystalloid casings. We simply modulate the degree of collective molecular imagination generated by the universe. Thus we can transport—and be transported—through so-called Time—and always be the first to arrive at good parties that we never have to leave. In any case this is all rather boring, and I am sure impenetrable to your teeny-tinies as well."

Uncle Nancy made a face. "I still don't understand what that has to do with hippies! And how in hell do I get my bar back?"

Bill scratched his crotch with grim depression. He hadn't the slightest idea what was happening or what they were talking about. And even worse, when he could get the next drink.

"Even through your fog of temporal confusion I see some meaning," philosophised Elliot. "Meaning penetrates and I understand now! Somehow, the hippies understood this on a preconscious level . . . and hypothesized your existence. They didn't exactly summon you as we had to. They calculated that for some reason you'd be here at a certain hour, minute, second and that you'd be open for the exact leap they needed . . . to wherever that was! Thus the agent was able to go back in Time and change history."

"But why this Nazi stuff?" asked Uncle Nancy. "That hardly jibes with my understanding of essential hippie philosophy."

"We can puzzle that out later!" said Elliot. "Right now, we have to go back and undo the damage that bearded bowb did." He spun to face the Time Portal. "Dudley . . . Sir, if I may make the supposition that that is your honorable title."

"Why yes, indeed it is!" the Time Portal simpered, pleased with this crafty bit of bumsucking.

"All you need to do is open your Portal again just as it was when the hippie leaped and allow us to jump through! In that way, we can go back and undo the damage!"

"Damage? Again, I see no damage. In truth I suppose the long and short of it is, Mr. Elliot Methadrine, Time Cop—and I must be insistent on this point—what's in it for me?"

"Well, I have a couple of megabucks I brought for expenses."

"Ah! Excellent! Far more than the hippie paid me!

Let's have a look at this money, and then I'll see about this adjustment."

Elliot took out the shining discs, the cross-eyed semblance of the Emperor glowing from each of them. A cash-register drawer 'chinged!' open from the alienoid interior of the Time Portal and swallowed up the offering.

"Super! Now then, my part of the bargain. Just allow me a few moments for a bit of concentration!" Antennae extended, quivering. Static electricity crackled between Van Der Graf generatorlike coils. Dollar and cent signs erupted from the portion that held the cash register.

"My God! He's doing it!" cried Uncle Nancy, pointing as Time mists poured through the glowing hole.

Bill looked. Sure enough in the moil and particolored fractious fantasy uncoiling within the Time Portal, Bill was able to see an image—a Time Ghost, if you will—of that hippie from Hellworld leaping through the space between Now and some other Then and disappearing in a twinkle of stars.

"Yes!" cried Elliot. "That's it! That's the instant! Hold that thought!" He turned to Bill and Uncle Nancy. "Well, guys! The Moment of Truth! Are you with me?"

"Uh," said Uncle Nancy, grinning artificially. "I'm just a simple barkeep. It is my duty I think to ... maybe I could do with some aerobic exercise! Maybe pump some iron! A few laps around the pool! You guys stay in touch, hear. Let me know how all this comes out." The bartender shuffled backwards, grinning smarmily.

"Whatever," said Elliot. "Come on, Bill. Let's show the universe some *real men in action!*"

"You know," said Bill inarticulately, "I've been kind of, you know, feeling poorly lately. Maybe a month's training would put me in better shape for this kind of particular mission."

". . . maybe they'll hire me to push their kumquat yogurt coolers!" came Uncle Nancy's voice, drifting back from the door.

"Kumquat yogurt coolers!" The very notion put a halt to Bill's intended departure. It stopped him long enough for Elliot to grab him.

"Come Trooper! Let's start earning the Emperor's bucks!"

The next thing Bill knew, Elliot Methadrine had hurled him straight into the maw of the Time Portal.

CHAPTER 8

BILL WAS FAMILIAR WITH THE CONCEPT OF *failing upward*. Certainly his graduation to his present position in the Troopers showed that this was basic to the law of bureaucratic mobility. However, never before had he ever had the sensation of *falling upward*—which was exactly what it felt like; what was happening now.

Nor was it remotely like drifting in zero gravity.

No, it was as though the universe had suddenly turned around 180 degrees and he'd been pushed off some cliff and was headed up, not down, at a steadily accelerating speed toward ominous rocks above. Rocks that felt like they were below.

Wobbly stomach, butterfly brain—rushing of air, smell of rotting gym bag, scream of fear.

Then, at the last moment, the rocks veered away

and Time itself came hurtling into this meaningless maelstrom.

And then Bill struck the ground—soft as the foamiest feather.

For the briefest of moments, he seemed to lose consciousness, and when he awoke it was with the light-headed feeling as though he were recovering from a faint. Which was a hell of a lot better, actually, than waking up from a massive hangover, or waking up dead, but was still disorienting.

Where the bowb was he anyway, Bill pondered puzzledly as he looked around.

He seemed to be in some sort of valley, surrounded by a vista of pine-topped mountains.

A bright sun shone hot and fiery and merciless in an infinitely azure sky.

The ground he was on was dry, fringed with scatterings of brown grass and spattered with stands of beautiful flowering saguaro cacti.

A desert! He was in some kind of desert. He felt around for a canteen, hoping that there was something cold and liquidly alcoholic inside. No canteen, no beer. Oh, well. Hadn't he read in his favorite book, his bible, A HEAVY DRINKER'S GUIDE TO HEAVY DRINKING, that tequila was made out of a kind of cactus? Plenty of the latter around. Must be a few bottles at least of the former.

But before Bill could begin his traditional search for drink, he was distracted by a sudden thump and a startled "Ooff!"

He turned to find Elliot Methadrine facefirst in a pile of sand, rear end prickly from an unfortunate run-in with a cactus limb on the way down.

"Ouch!" expostulated Elliot, slowly climbing to

his feet and twisting his head around to try and inspect his rear. Gingerly, he began pulling the spikes from their pincushion placement.

"Yow! You must have a high pain threshold!" said Bill, cringing with posterial empathy at the spectacle. "Me, I'd like a strong drink before I tried that." He turned around and looked at where they'd landed. "You know, Elliot, I'm afraid I don't see a whole lot of history that can be changed around here!"

Elliot ploinked the last cactus needle from his backside, then looked about doubtfully. "You haven't seen that hippie around here, then."

"No. All I see are those pretty guano birds hovering up there. Maybe they're the intelligent aliens of this planet and they're here to greet us."

"No, Bill," said Elliot. "Those are buzzards. I'm afraid they're waiting for us to die so they can eat us. Beak straight up the arse and soft guts first. Eyeballs for dessert."

"Don't talk like that!" Bill quavered, then looked back up at the hovering things with alarm. "That's not the way I want to die. In fact—I don't want to die at all! Anyway, where the hell are we, Elliot? Have you got a clue? And when you get the clue—what do we do?"

"I'm not totally sure, but it looks a hell of a lot like Duneworld or Desertplanet or, if you can believe the holohistories, a desert back on long-gone-but-never-forgotten Earth. You know what would be real nice right about now?"

"A beer . . . no, two beers. Make that three beers!"

"Shut up, Bill. I could use a talk with that Time Portal, Dudley Do-Do."

"Maybe he'll bring us a six-pack," Bill said doubtfully. Already, that scorching sun was getting hot on the back of his neck and he could feel his sensitive scalp broiling under the heavy-duty burner heat waves that sizzled him.

"Did I indeed hear my honored name being taken in vain, gentlemen?" came that proper British accent.

Bill and Elliot spun around.

There, in a spot judiciously distant from prickly cactus plants, materialized none other than the aforementioned Sir Dudley. In a halo of shimmering lights the Time Portal dipped into this particular reality.

"Speak!" Bill cozened. "Where the hell are we?"

"Is this where that hippie went?" demanded Elliot.

The crystalline array of controls inside the Portal winked and blipped and danced to a tune curiously similar to the Colonel Bogie march. The TV set flashed images of historical periods, then seemed to get stuck for an endless period on a monumentally dull cricket match.

The Portal was mute then for a suspiciously long period of time.

"Dudley?" said Elliot. "Sir Dudley. We presume you are checking your controls to answer our question?"

"Hmm? No, actually I was watching England playing India. Damned foreigners are thrashing us. Pardon me?"

"You're supposed to be checking on that hippie who's changed the universe!"

"Well, you'll have to excuse me, but cricket hasn't changed a jot! Longest, most boring game really, cricket. Gets in the blood though. That is, it would get in my blood if I had any. An intellectual sport perhaps—"

"Shut up!" Bill hinted as he scratched his cooking head, burning his fingers in the process. "I don't want to hear about games—I want to hear about out of here!"

The Time Portal, rapt and fascinated by its monologue, ignored him. "I have thought a lot about the game of cricket. It's eternal, so it doesn't really count as a game. But back to that hippie bounder, eh?" The lights began their antic parade once more, finally flashing all at once in a climactic paroxysm. A John Philip Soused march (Bill's favorite) sounded from the speakers.

"You've found him! You've found him!" said Bill.

"Well, frankly, no, I haven't. Curious. Seems to be a bit of a commotion back at Central."

"Central?"

"Yes. The Paradox Processor seems to be overloading. Oh dear, I'm being summoned back!"

Sir Dudley the Time Portal began to tremble and shake. Then, slowly, he began to fade into thin air.

"Wait! Come back!" cried Elliot.

"At least leave us something to drink!" cried Bill.

"Sorry, gentlemen! I shall make every effort to return. I do hope you survive on this godforsaken—"

And then, with an imploding *plop* the Time Portal plopped out of existence. An arid wind whined mournfully in his place, stirring up a dust devil—and then all was still.

Elliot shook his head. "Damn! If that doesn't beat all! The bastard didn't even bother to tell us where the hell we are. Not the place, the year, the date, the time... absolutely nothing. We can only presume that somehow this is the place where that hippie went. And this is where he changed Time, the future and the past. Where he did the dirty deed that we must reverse."

"What about that Time Ticker of yours, Mr. Time Cop?" asked Bill.

"Ah, yes. Little problem with that item!" Elliot pointed down. The mechanism was on the ground, dial faces cracked, obviously inoperative.

"Well, at least you can try and fix it!" said Bill, screaming with incredulity. "I mean, we've got to do something to find out where we are!"

Elliot was staring off into the distance. "Hmm. I believe we are about to experience a valuable clue into that matter, friend Bill."

"Clue?" Bill turned around in the direction Elliot was facing. Sure enough, approaching them was a rooster-tail of dust.

And the cause of that upraised dust was definitely not roosters, though Bill and Elliot would certainly have cause to wish they had been, later.

CHAPTER 9

THEY CAME IN A CLATTERING OF HOOVES
and a flurry of war whoops, an advancing effluvium
of poorly dried animal skins, horse puckey and buffalo chips wafting out before them.

They rode strange and ferocious four-legged animals that Bill recognized from WESTERN HIS-
TORICAL HORROR comix as being gorses or
horses or something like that. The warriors mounted
on the gorses' backs—or was it morses?—had eyes
that were glaring wild, while their faces and bodies
were streaked with war paint. Trailing backward in
the wind were feathered headdresses like proud animal manes, flashing brilliantly in the sun.

Ca—rack!

Something whooshed close to Bill's ear.

Woo-HOOOOOSH!

Pointed feather shafts hurtled past them, burying

their barbed heads in the sand or thunking into cactus.

"Arrows!" screamed Elliot. "They're shooting arrows at us, Bill!"

"Bullets with feathers!" howled Bill, already turned about-face and starting on the first footfall of a frantic run. "They're shooting feathered bullets at us, Elliot!"

With a clatter of hoofbeats, the pursuing war party sprinted the few remaining yards, splitting in two as they did so to surround the fleeing time travelers. Bill found himself suddenly confronted by a pair of fierce-eyed savages, pointing particularly sharp-looking lances at them.

Bill thought it wise to stop in his tracks and throw up his arms in immediate surrender. Elliot did likewise, but added the even wiser maneuver of falling on his knees in total and abjectly quivering defeat.

Seeing that this was the best of all possible recourses in their present hopeless situation, Bill tumbled as well.

The wild-eyed savages hauled on the reins of their steeds, pulling up just short of the visitors. The lances were not withdrawn however; rather, Bill, to his extreme discomfort, found a razor-sharp length of steel attempting frontier barber duty at his throat.

"Ugh!" said a commanding voice behind them.

"I thought so," said Elliot, having difficulty talking, since an identical length of metal had been jabbed next to his throat. "Indians!"

"You mean, the kind that were playing cricket against Sir Dudley's team?" said Bill.

"No, no, Bill. Red Indians. North American plains Indians of nineteenth-century, lost-but-not-forgotten, Earth! I don't wish to brag, but I did rather well in history in Time School."

"How do you know for sure?"

"We appear to be somewhere in an unpopulated area of the American Southwest, these guys sure look like something out of my favorite John Whine movie, FORT SCROFULA—and besides, 'Ugh' is a definite Indian word of surly greeting."

"Utter rubbish," said the same voice. "I was merely expressing my extreme disgust at your repulsive presences!"

Bill turned around.

Standing tall in his saddle was a particularly noble-looking redskin, his chest puffed out in a haughty manner. He had a powerful frame, large biceps wrapped in ceremonial leather straps and studs, hung with claws and teeth of long-dead carnivores. Bill had seen his type in bars, and he could usually best him in a bar brawl, since noble sorts tended to fight fair and Bill's brawling was definitely of the dirty and underhanded variety. However, all the rifles and aimed arrows, to say nothing of the razor blade beneath his chin, prevented Bill from any notion of fighting at the moment.

"Oh," said Bill, showing his very best buttocks-bussing smile. "Hi! Great skin-paint job," he smarmed. "Nifty clothes. Who's your tailor?"

"I should ask you the identical question!" grunted the Indian. "I have never seen such garb before, and I am a graduate of Harvard." He scratched his head. "Or was that Yale! I confess, this blasted sun has been getting to me lately! Buffalo Billabong! My medicine!"

"Yes, oh Chief Thunder Bluster!" yapped a short, stocky man, wearing a nine-and-a-half-gallon hat with an ostrich feather stuffed in the top and corks dangling from bits of string all around the rim, as he stumped up to his master's horse. Around the medicine's man shoulder was hung a pouch, and from the puffy leather thing he drew out a bottle of sickly green fluid. "Here·you go, cobber. And g'day, lads! And by the way, Chiefie—that was Kalamazoo Business Institute where you got your chief's skin." The red-nosed man then pulled himself up a gigantic can of Foster's lager and sprayed the assembled mightily as he opened it. "Oh well. Another one of these to'dai will probably make me chunder. But what the bloody hell!"

The man lifted beer to lips and guzzled, his Adam's apple and his corks bobbing with equal enthusiasm.

Bill's eyes bugged. Boy, he wanted that beer! However, more than even beer, Bill desired to keep his carotid artery unsevered and to prevent his blood from spurting willy-nilly about the desert floor.

"You see what I mean, Bill!" said Elliot. "A classic Indian medicine man! I estimate that we must indeed be in the American Southwest—oh, about 1885, I'd say!"

"Again I must inquire," said Chief Thunder Bluster. "Who are you? Quickly, before I slice open your bellies for those vultures' antipasto!"

"We are travelers in time, oh Great Chief! Servants of Truth and Right and Great Tonto Fans!" said Elliot in his most obsequious tone.

"We're looking for a dirty, hairy hippie back here who wants to change the very fabric of time from 100 percent cotton to 50 percent polyester and 50 percent rayon!" said Bill, and instantly shook his head and wondered why he had said it. The heat! It was getting him.

"Yes, and the entire Universe of the future has

turned Nazi and only I, Elliot Methadrine, and my boon companion Bil—"

"That's with two Ls."

"—only two-L'ed Bill and I can save it by apprehending that history-hammering hippie. Now then Chief... what do you say? You don't want to see a universe dominated by goose-stepping sausage suckers, do you? To say nothing of foul-smelling zoned-out herbiage-smoking rebels?"

"50 percent polyester and 50 percent rayon!" said Chief Thunder Bluster. "Why, that's the exact content of my wigwam!"

"That's far out!" husked the medicine man, downing one of the buzzards with his empty Foster's can. "In fact," he continued as he pulled out a huge peace pipe and tamped great amounts of suspiciously green shag into the bowl, "I should say it's bloody well cosmic, mates!"

"Gee—" sottoed Elliot, sotto voce to his companion. "You don't think, Bill, that the hippie might have come back to score some grass and accidentally changed history?"

"I think I'd like to score one of those beers, myself," Bill said hoarsely.

"Say, noble Chief," Elliot whined invitingly. "Why don't we take this pow-wow back to that bargain wigwam of yours, perhaps share a view of your brews and talk this over mano a red mano!"

"Silence!" ordered the Chief. "In a word—no! Since we do not know what is to be done with you strange dung-beings from Beyond, then we must bring it before Higher Authority!"

"Ah! You mean there's a delegation of the United States Cavalry here then!" said Elliot. "You know, Bill, my history teacher always said that the Cavalry always came to the rescue in these sort of tight spots back in the West. Except, of course, in the case of Custer's Last Stand.''

"Custard? Eating? Booze?" said one-thought-on-his-brain, maximum two, Bill.

"What I mean, repulsive strangers, is that we shall bring you up before the Altar of the Gods, where it shall be decided what shall be done with you!"

"Altar of the Gods," whimpered Elliot. "Sounds ominous."

With quick skill the savages hog-tied Bill and Elliot thoroughly, then started to drag them through the hot desert sand toward their date with the local deities.

All in all, Bill thought, an impressively depressing first day back in the past.

But then that wasn't precisely a surprise, since all of Bill's past was depressing.

Water splashed on Bill's face.

As much as he usually disdained the stuff, he found himself gulping at it automatically, to slake the mammoth thirst that engulfed him. For a moment he thought he was on some blissful pleasure planet, in bathing suit and water-wings, frolicking with water nymphs; such was the dementia that the baking sun had brought about. Ah yes! The resort of Blub-blub on the world of Glug; or perhaps even Splish-Splash Beach in the Snorkle-Dork system!

But no sooner had these gulps of water hauled him back up out of the depths of unconsciousness than Bill realized that not only was the sun beating down on him explicitly not of the vacation-resort variety, but that he was still stuck in this horrible desert in this wretched time, with the added burden of a good dozen cactus spines stuck in his nether parts.

"Ye—Ouch!" he said, blundering up to his feet, blinking and gasping. Well, it would seem that he'd been freed of his bonds, but that didn't necessarily mean anything wonderful. Bill wiped the water from his eyes and stumbled about, trying to get bearing and balance. "Elliot! Where are you, Elliot!" he called, trying to make out the parched environment with his bleared vision. He staggered forward a few yards, until he bumped into something . . . something hard. He heard a distinct hissing sound in stereo, and he thought maybe he'd bumped into some sort of motorized vehicle with two punctured tires. He stepped back so as not to get run over, and to get a better look at this obstacle.

Groaning, Bill wiped the water from his eyes. He looked up, and what stood before him was most emphatically not what he'd expected.

"Yikes!" said Bill, forgetting the pain of the cactus needles. For, rearing above him at a goodly height of ten feet was a monolithic creature of ghastly countenance. In fact, two countenances—and both of the heads looked like serpents or alligators or something else definitely Chingeroid.

Twin serpent tongues flickered out at ridiculous lengths. Glittering eyes stared down at Bill. Nor was this the last of the terrors this outrageously repulsive creature held. Its arms held out toward Bill ended in hands like scorpion tails. Great breasts like unholstered howitzers hung from the chest: whatever creature it was, it was female. In fact, it even wore some sort of skirt. A curious fashion statement indeed, the skirt appeared to consist entirely of living, curling snakes!

No, this female was not precisely the answer to his lustful prayers!

Bill staggered back, but tripped and fell. With a great snarling, threatening heave, the monster roared toward him.

"Don't eat me!" cried Bill. "I don't taste very good! Elliot! Help! Sir Dudley! Help! Anybody! Help!"

But Elliot and Sir Dudley did not respond, nor in fact did anybody come to the rescue. The monstrous thing rolled up to Bill, hovering.

"Who . . . Who are you?" asked Bill, squinting up at the thing, a bit blinded by the bright sun.

"My name," said the creature, "is Cue-tip the mighty Aztec God, who guards this valley and consumes anyone who dares venture anywhere near that highly significant secret cave yonder that leads to someplace mysterious and highly forbidden! And you?"

"Bill."

"Bill. A good and highly edible name." The two pair of eyes glittered like jewels in the sun. "Bill-thing . . . either you are very crazy to be here or the strong warriors of the Epoxy tribe have sent you down as a tasty sacrifice to get gulped down by my loathsome hungry self!"

"Actually, neither. I'm just—er—a friendly pilgrim in search of revelation. Thought maybe I would join your church. Religion, can't get too much of that. Any other god hereabouts besides your noble self?"

"So you seek religious succor. No way—you have to be born into the tribe. And there is no help from the others. Who include deities such as Phlegm—he's the one who favors chewing on beating hearts. And then there's Texaco, the condor beast; he likes to eat small human babies. And of course there's the noble king-god Coaxialcoitus, who devours the naked human maidens! Lots more minor deities, I suppose, but those are your basic pantheon, intruder. Now, if you'll be very still I'll just make short painful work instead of long drawn-out agony and you'll be my afternoon sacrificial supper, good and proper!"

Bill, however, had no intention of being anyone's supper, god or no god. "Look, I've got all these prickly things in me. I'll be quite rough going down your throat."

"No problem. I'll murder you first and pluck you later!" The Aztec god bellowed the words, advancing. The snakes hissed and the scorpion claws snapped.

Bill was motivated to backpedal.

"Stay still, for there is no escape from the gods," roared the creature. "How can I kill you if you keep scrabbling away from me?"

Keep her talking! The adrenalin-induced advice sizzled through Bill's brain cells. "But I seek guidance of the gods, great Cue-tip. Could you not reveal to a sinner exactly what's behind that door there?"

"What's behind the secret door? You mean, the door to the mysterious tunnel into an entirely different world? The one that I'm guarding? Well, I really can't tell you, now can I? That would be telling, and I'm here to guard the secret and—wait . . . hey, come back here! You tricked me! You didn't really want to know! You just wanted the chance to escape from me! I bet you taste rotten! You don't really deserve to be eaten by a god!"

"I'll tell you what you can eat, Cue-tip!"

Bill was tearing away by this time, skipping yards ahead of the thing, but happy to be alive, despite the severe discomfort the cactus spines were causing. Surprised, as always, at the amount of energy he was able to invest into the continuation of his imminent personal survival, Bill tore up a long wide arroyo, strained his way up the slope, made a Herculean leap over the top, and even as he did he was gratified to hear the hissing and rattling of the guard-god Cue-tip receding behind him. He rolled down a dusty hill on the other side, gasping and heaving breaths.

And banged smack into a pair of legs. "Good grief," said a too-familiar voice. "You're supposed to have been gobbled up quite thoroughly by now!"

Bill looked up. His heart and his bowels sank. Standing before him was Chief Thunder Bluster, his men behind him with their previous complement of fearsome, deadly weapons.

"This one's a crafty cobber, sir!" intoned Buffalo Billabong, the tribe's medicine man. "Cue-tip had her chance, as prescribed. May I suggest that we add another log to that sacrificial fire."

Bill sighed as his head slammed into the dirt. He definitely didn't like the sound of that.

Talk about out of the frying pan . . .

CHAPTER **10**

... AND INTO THE FIRE!

"Another fine mess!" said Elliot. "That's getting
to be the story of my life!"

Elliot Methadrine was tied to a round stake stuck
into the ground. Bill, much to his dismay, was tied
to the other side of that same stake. His feet were
slowly being covered by mesquite logs carried up to
the imminent bonfire by a brace of squaws.

"Sir Dudley will come back for us!" gulped Bill,
trying to con himself into some hope. "And what's
the chance of your Time Central boys homing in on
our whereabouts!"

"We're a needle in a Timestack, Bill. They'll never
find us!" moaned Elliot. "And I'm afraid I haven't
got much faith in Sir Dudley!"

"So what do we do, then?" Bill asked.

"Attempt to reason with these savages, I suppose,"

sighed Elliot. "Although I must say they seem terribly intent upon this little heathen fricassee! Though it's nice to have company, I'm sorry to see you here. When they took you first, they howled something about using you as a token sacrifice to some minor deity or something."

Bill briefly outlined the events as they had occurred.

"Hmm. Most curious," said Elliot. "A secret tunnel, you say, guarded by some sort of reptilian-oriented creature of the Aztec persuasion. You know, Bill, there's definitely something about this environment that bothers me. I mean, something about the place that just doesn't quite spell 'Arizona, late nineteenth century' to me."

Bill, who knew little about history—and cared even less—nervously eyed the squaw carrying a fresh batch of firewood toward him. Sure enough, she dumped a hefty chunk of mesquite directly on his big toe. Bill suppressed a scream, asking his question through gritted teeth: "Isn't there something pretty strange too with that giant doorstop over there?"

The structure Bill referred to was a stone pyramid perhaps forty feet high, runneled with drying blood and decorated with human hearts, grinning skulls and funeral wreaths with faded ribbons.

"No, no, Bill. All the Indians had those."

"You mean, the medicine man with the strange accent drinking Foster's lager?"

"No, no, Bill. Medicine men were important fixtures of Western Indian culture."

Bill tried to scratch his head, but couldn't. "Look, could you hold the historical lecture for a bit and think of a way out of this?"

"I find it most fascinating. In many ways this seems

to be a perfect representation in all respects of the American West. But there are anomalies."

"Like the horses?"

"Your education was severely limited and your vocabulary borders on the nonexistent. Not animals, pinhead. Anomalies are things that do not adhere to a coherent pattern. Such as, I've got problems with that sky. It's not quite right."

"The sky? You mean, like how it's green."

"No, Bill. It's only green because you appear to be colorblind as well. No, it's that blasted sun."

"Whew. It is hot. But even a moron like me, El-liot," Bill sneered, trying to get some points back, "even without a vocabulary, knows that most suns are hot. I didn't have to go to no college, like some people, to know that!"

"Now look at whose little ego got rubbed the wrong way! Yes, of course most suns are hot, Bill. But have you noticed the way that one wobbles?"

"Don't all suns wobble?"

"Only when you drink all the time."

Bill ignored the insult and peeked at the sun through slitted eyes. "Maybe—yes. And it stops and it starts again. And sometimes it goes back and forth, like it can't make up its mind whether it wants to keep on going west or it wants to back up and set back in the east."

"I'm not entirely sure if what we're talking about is astronomically possible, Bill."

Before Bill could waste much time brooding over this, the Chief arrived, along with his medicine man and a number of sinister-looking redskins carrying torches.

"Right," said Buffalo Billabong, spewing another keg-sized can of Foster's all over the place as he opened it. A few tantalizing drops fell upon Bill's pants leg, but alas, none in his mouth. "G'day, maytes. Today we play Morton Bay bugs on the barbie, right?"

"Is that entirely necessary?" whined Elliot. "Surely you'd prefer it if we bribed you with some wampum, right?"

"You wouldn't have any firewater, would you?" asked Bill, making feeble connections at last with his memories of his copies of ROARING KINKY WESTERN COWBOYS AND TRANSVESTITE INJUNS THREE DEE COMIX.

"Just what are you idiots talking about?" demanded Chief Thunder Bluster. "Would you speak English for heaven's sake and not that pagan nonsense?"

"But that's what you're doing now—a pagan ceremony, correct?" responded Elliot.

"Well of course," snarled Thunder Bluster. "How do you expect us to appease the heathen gods with anything less than a pagan ceremony? You don't think that they would be very impressed if we attempted to baptize you, do you?"

"Why don't you give it a try?" suggested Bill.

"Well, actually, this is going to be a very sweet and pleasant ceremony and not at all within our realm of bloodthirsty tradition," said Buffalo Billabong. "No, I think a cookout is of an entirely more appropriate nature, don't you? The gods will not only be appeased, they can have spareribs for dinner!" He pulled out a book from his hip pocket even as he sipped at his huge can of Foster's. His lips moved as he read the greasy-paged book, the corks on his hat bobbling in the midst of a cloud of flies.

"And I suppose that's a collection of implorations to the gods!" said Elliot. "Don't you see the entire thing is ridiculous? There are no gods! It looks as though your superstitious tribe are the victims of—"

"Stuff it, buster!" said Chief Thunder Bluster, "or I'll stuff a live prairie dog down your gob!"

The threat was enough to keep Elliot silenced effectively, and Bill as well. Particularly since the chief waved over his prairie dog handler with a couple of fat specimens and shook them in their direction with sinister intent.

"Bravo!" commented the medicine man, observing all this. He held up the book. Upon the leather jacket was inscribed, SERVING BLOODTHIRSTY PAGAN GODS GOOD. "Actually, it's a recipe book! Let's see . . . Upchuckandpeck, the big god around here—"

"I thought it was Coaxialcoitus!" said Bill. "That's what you told us earlier."

"Oh yes . . . so it is. There you go, mate. You see, you'll get a bit of education before you snuff it. Wrong recipe." He paged around until he found the appropriate one. "Well, well, well. Looks as though the dread and holy Coaxial is a man after my own heart—as well as after all the hearts of the sacrifices we rip out around this place. He prefers his meals marinated in Foster's lager!"

Bill's ears perked up. "Beer?"

"That's right, mayte!" Buffalo Billabong put his fingers into his mouth and whistled. Immediately a whole cartload of Foster's Lager cans were trundled in with great ceremony, dispatch and racket.

Bill's mouth started watering. He watched with unmoving attention as a pair of Indian braves opened a pair of beer cans and then stepped forward, faces intent with seriousness, muttering strange ceremonial words like "Schlitz", "Budweiser" and "Ole Froth-ingslosh, the Pale Stale Ale" under their breaths. Per-haps these Indians, Bill thought, were not as savage as Elliot had originally thought.

He closed his eyes and opened his mouth expect-antly.

Instead of pouring the beer into his mouth, how-ever, the Indians poured it over his head. It ran down his hair and ears, soaked into his shirt. At first he spluttered, then began to suck desperately at the run-nels of brew coming down his face, only managing to extract the odd tantalizing sip.

When the can was empty, Bill opened his eyes. "Say, you know, Buff, I think some inside marinat-ing would help!"

"Stop this nonsense! Get on with the lighting of the pyre," roared the chief. "Burn these idiots! The great god grows impatient."

"No, no, wait . . ." said the medicine man. "Per-haps he's right, Chief. That's not a bad idea."

"Oh, if you must. After all, you are the medicine man around here and there is such a thing as protocol. But be quick about it! You can't expect the gods to hang around all day waiting for a sacrifice."

Bill sighed happily. At least he'd get a drink or two before he had to face the flames. Still and all, it wasn't exactly something he was looking forward to. He watched as the Indian braves pried open Elliot's mouth and poured in a can of Foster's.

When the beer can came to Bill's mouth, he glugged it down in a single giant insufflation. This impressed the Indians so greatly that they decided they needed to pour another can down his gullet. Bill had no complaint of course, accepting it gladly, guz-zling it quickly. However, after the third and the fourth cans he found it was getting a bit harder to take the beer, and on the sixth, with his belly painfully extended, he discovered that he was not only getting drunk, which was an okay thing, but he was also getting positively uncomfortable.

Bill then managed to burble the words that he never imagined he would say in his entire alcoholic life. "I think—blub!—that's enough beer . . ."

"I couldn't agree more!" said the chief. "Let's move this thing on! I want to see these paleskins well roasted. The gods must be propitiated! Let the barbecue begin!"

Bill belched contentedly. He was so marinated by now that he didn't really care. Elliot, however, who'd only been able to take a single can of Foster's, began to plead for his life, giving sound arguments for his release, appealing to their sense of honor and asking them what their mothers would think about a sacrifice like this. None of this impressed the Indians in any way.

"Now then, that's done," said Buffalo Billabong, nodding his head at the preparations and feeling through his pockets. "Hmm. Who's got the matches and the lighter fluid?"

"Here. Use mine!" said Chief Thunder Bluster obligingly, pulling out a can labeled Zippo Bar-B-Que fluid, as well as a disposable lighter.

"Right!" The medicine man grabbed the lighter fluid and squirted it on the mesquite wood around Bill's and Elliot's feet. "You know, maytes, this won't be so bad. You'll be crisped in just a flash. Then we'll salt and spice you up proper like, plenty of garlic, put some parsley around you and serve you up to the gods."

Bill, thoroughly squiffed on Foster's lager, consid-

INTERMISSION

EXCITING—

—isn't it? But you don't want to get too carried away, chewing your fingernails and such. Nor should you read this book so closely that you drag your eyeballs across the page, which tends to make them red and irritated. To ease the strain, we now bring you an ART SECTION!

Didn't expect that, did you? Advanced technology and a hyperspace viewer has permitted Mark Pacella to actually project upon the screen in his studio views of the action in this book. Working like crazy—since the images fade in seconds—he has made sketches of these events to later be turned into the polished master-drawings you see here.

So kindly turn the page to see...

A very realistic hologram of what a deadly Chinger is supposed to look like. And, if you want to know, that *is* real blood on its claws.

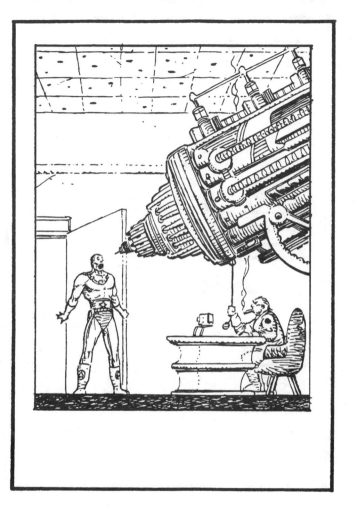

Well, yes—Bill is a hero, not a coward. But don't you think any one of us would look very much the same with a laser cannon pushed down the throat?

Heart in throat and fleet of foot, Bill just makes it off the transport to a planet of certain doom. Great!

Here is something we never thought we would see. Bill, the perpetual Private acting as officer. It brings a tear to the eye, not to mention a dribble to the tusk.

Bebop and boogie, Daddy-O! This grotty and grungy horrible hippy is definitely a mean mother with a distinct fascination for assassination!

Heap bad news for Bill. These smiling and friendly ever-welcoming aborigines have a warm reception in mind for him. Turn the page and you will see...

It's going to be a hot time in the old teepee tonight. Is it to roast Bill on the stake?

This janitor is ahead of his time—or perhaps two heads are better than one. How heady a job this really is!

A welcome four-armed, green-tailed, well-armed, bad-breathed Chinger to the rescue!

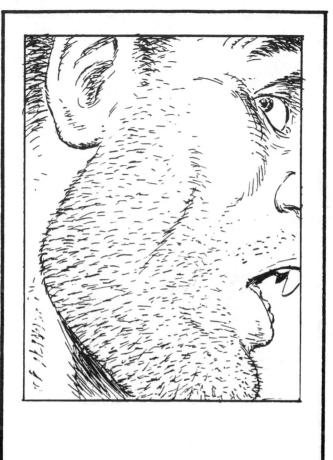

Now here is something that you don't see every day—
nor would you want to. An earlobe implant that is not
only smarter than the ear, but smarter than Bill as well.
Which, unhappily, doesn't take much.

It was no pleasure cruise. After two years chained to the wall in the prison ship, Bill not only needs a shave and a haircut—but a good steam-cleaning as well.

What ales him now? Never a heel, old lager and leave
'er Bill tries to foot the bar tab.

E N D   O F
I N T E R M I S S I O N

ered death. He wondered, how can I die if I haven't been born yet? It didn't seem possible. Besides, Bill had never died before, so he didn't really know what to expect. There were times before that he'd almost died, but he'd been only half-crocked then as opposed to now when he was fully crocked.

Staring at the flaming lighter, Bill considered life and death. All in all, he was just as happy to go out now, if not in a blaze of glory, then at least a blaze. Tanked up on brew, brain flying high, visions of Avalon, Valhalla, Olympus, the Holy Bar and Grill dancing willy-nilly in his noodle—Joan of Arc, watch out. Here comes Bill of Spark! he thought.

However, even as the trembling flame neared the kindling, Bill noticed from the corner of his eye that a curious cloud was putt-putting toward them from the horizon, a little bilious blimp scooting along in the sky. Clouds, of course, were normally nothing to get excited about, but thus far Bill had seen absolutely none here in the southwestern past of North America. Also, (he blinked to make sure) it seemed to be scudding along at a goodly clip, directly toward them as though a cloud on a mission.

Bill's interest in the cloud vanished instantly, however, when, with a wicked crackling and whoosh of flame, things started to get a little hot.

He looked down in horror to see that the lighter had successfully touched the tinder, and flames were not only licking the wood, but were singeing and crisping his boots in a decidedly unpleasant manner.

"Oh . . . Oh . . . No, please, I beg of you noble aborigines!" cried Elliot. "I'm too young to die! There are missions yet to be fulfilled, women to be loved—"

"—beer to be drunk," agreed Bill. "Don't burn me either." He pleaded, searching for something appropriate to say, but found himself vacant of any inspiration other than losing his temper. "You bowbs will live to regret this!" Which wasn't very impressive and only drew sneers from the redskins.

The flames roared higher.

The smiles on the Red Indians' faces grew wider, and they started to do a wild dance to celebrate the delicious conflagration.

But something remarkable was about to happen. Something as inappropriate and impossible as a lawyer going to heaven.

The Indians beat tom-toms and worked themselves up into a hysterical lather, too high to notice the cloud stealing over them until it was too late.

With a crack of ear-destroying thunder, a ministorm broke. Water rained down upon the mesquite fire, drowning it out with much smoky hissing and gurgling. A bolt of lightning frizzled down, striking one of the redskins and blasting him right out of his moccasins.

"Hark! It comes upon me that, perhaps, there is a message of some kind here!" intoned Chief Thunder Bluster. "I do think that this seems to be some sort of sign from the gods."

Bill was happy it was a sign from somebody. This little fire had almost put paid to any ambitions he might have had regarding progeny.

"Bollocks!" cried the frustrated medicine man. "Talk about raining on the parade! What did we do wrong, oh gods, that you should rain out our holy barbie in this manner?"

"Bill!" shouted Elliot. "Look!"

Bill looked.

Sure enough, there was something remarkable to look at.

"You're right! There are still full cans of Foster's lager on that cart!"

"No, you quasi-alcoholic military moron, no!" screamed Elliot. "Not the beer. The cloud! Look at the cloud."

Bill blinked his eyes and tried to focus his attention on the cloud. He saw that the vapors of which it was composed were moving—moving and moiling so as to form a face!

The face had a big clown nose, protruding clown eyes and frizzy red hair, with a painted-on frown. "Hark and honk!" said the clown god, honking a horn from within its little cumuloid assemblage of water vapor. "I am Quetzelbozo, the clown of ridiculous blood-thirsty pagan Aztec ceremony. I've been sent by Coaxialcoitus to tell you that you're doing this all wrong."

"Wrong!" said Buffalo Billabong. "Why, we've got them marinated to high heaven!"

The clown-god sniffed. "Yeah. I can smell them from here. But you didn't do the rituals right. Recipe seems right on, but the rituals we gods like have to be included to make it a proper sacrifice."

"Oh, damn! Of course! I forgot the pies!" said the medicine man.

"That's right!" said the clown-god. "Prerequisite to the proper ritual burning of sacrificial victims is a proper mashing of cream pies in the face!"

"That's about as bad as a poke in the eye with a burnt stick!" moaned the medicine man, slapping his forehead in self-abasement and derision. "I forgot the cream pies." He fell down to his knees before the clown-cloud. "What else has your humble, penitent servant forgotten, your Big-noseship?"

"The rubber chicken with its head bitten off!"

Buffalo Billabong's eyes went wide. "The rubber chook—of course! How could I have possibly forgotten the bloody chook! This is just not my flipping day."

"You got it that time, buster. Be prepared to take your punishment for absentmindedness, worthless servant."

The medicine man braced himself and closed his eyes. A spray of carbonated water squirted from the cloud, smacking him on the kisser, followed by a dead mackerel which slapped him wetly in the forehead.

Holy blood-thirsty laughter echoed through the canyons. Even Bill and Elliot had to laugh. This was better than dying, thought Bill. Now if they could escape—along with some more drink—everything would be pretty all right.

Buffalo Billabong sighed and gestured to the nearest Indian brave to go and procure the important items he had forgotten.

Meanwhile, Bill felt something around the vicinity of his wrists. There was a momentary constriction, and then he found his bonds falling at his feet.

"Huh?" said Bill.

"Shh!" said Elliot. "The fire and the soaking loosened the bonds. Don't move—and don't run until I do."

"You're on!"

"Pardon me, Mr. Quetzelbozo," Elliot said, "but I have an important philosophical question to ask you."

"Let me guess," said the cloud. "You want to know whether the universe is really perched on the back of a turtle held up by giant elephants?"

"Close but not quite on."

"Knock it off, buster—I'm not playing twenty questions with some prospective roast. What is it?"

"The answer to a very simple question. If you gods are so great how come you let the entire U.S. cavalry over there come and break up this rotten ritual?"

In unison every head—including the god's—turned towards the dusty plains.

Elliot and Bill threw off their bonds and ran as though their lives depended on it. Which, of course, they did.

CHAPTER 11

BILL'S REAR END WAS SINGED. HIS STOM-ach, filled with beer, sloshed and swung back and forth as he ran, panting and gasping, with Elliot gasping and panting and trundling along at his side. There were arrows zipping past his ears, lightning bolts from the clown god cracking at his feet, and off to one side just what they didn't need: that damned Cue-tip thing, snarling and hissing, coming toward them looking extremely on the bad-tempered side.

All in all, Bill wondered, close to exhaustion, if maybe he hadn't been better off back in the middle of that sacrificial fire, bombed out of his gourd on Foster's lager and about to be booted out of life well before he'd even been born.

"The doorway to the tunnel!" cried Elliot, dodging an arrow. "Where'd you say that doorway was?"

Bill—stumbling, cursing, and in the act of dodging an arrow himself—was hard-pressed to answer.

"There's that other damned Aztec god, Bill!" moaned Elliot. "You said the doorway was somewhere near the lizard god, so where is it? Hurry up, man, or if the Indians don't get us, that monster will!"

Bill could see that Elliot was quite correct. Cue-tip, mightily peeved and hissing with joy upon seeing the man who had just escaped its jaws within its sights again, roared and snarled and trundled toward them, obviously bent upon Bill's total destruction, mastication, digestion and undoubtedly elimination in more ways than one.

"The tunnel!" said Bill. "Right! It's over there!" His pointing finger wobbled as he tried to point in the direction where he'd seen that mysterious opening to the other world alluded to by Cue-tip.

"Bill!" cried Elliot. "I don't see it!" He cried desperately, recoiling as he ran—which is very hard to do. "I DON'T SEE IT BUT I DO SEE THAT GOD, AND THAT MONSTER IS HUGE!"

Sure enough, the saliva-dripping jaws of Cue-tip, to say nothing of the hissing rattlesnake kirtle and the scorpion-tail claws, were nearing them with extreme rapidity.

"Kill them!" ordered Thunder Bluster. "Shoot them!"

Another volley of arrows tore through the air. Bill did not exactly duck this time, though the consequence of the next event served the same purpose: he tripped. He tripped on a rock, and in doing so managed to knock Elliot Methadrine down as well. But good fortune doth come. Occasionally. For they both went down in a tumble, and the just-released hail of arrows tore through the airspace they had just occupied, banging and thunking into various parts of the anatomy of the Aztec god called Cue-tip.

Now it is written that even monsters of legendary nature are supposed to have been of flesh and blood, or something disgusting roughly resembling flesh and blood, so when Bill looked up he expected Cue-tip to be at least bleeding a little bit—and hopefully mortally or immortally wounded.

Instead, he was startled to see the Aztec god going through strong reactions of a decidedly electronic nature.

One of its lizard heads had been blown clear off, exposing wires and computer components. Most of the arrows had bounced off its chest, but the ones that had connected were now fountaining showers of sparks. The snakes wiggled and squirmed, bolts of static electricity snapping between them.

"Argh! Zap! Snap! Crackle! Pop!" crackled Cue-tip. "Kill the infidels! Bowb the Emperor! Fie Fi Fo Fum Fizzle!"

It then slowly keeled over, spasming and spuming fire and sparks, to hit the ground with a decidedly metallic crash.

"You aboriginal Indian idiots!" cried Chief Bluster. "You shot the god."

"This I do believe," moaned Buffalo Billabong, "Is what might be called in the old outback definitely bad news!"

"Infidels!" exhorted the clown-cloud god, zipping over on its cloud. "They must not be allowed to escape. My wrath is mighty, let me tell you, and there are going to be some roasted redskins around here if—"

It was an ungodly sight, for the god never finished

its goddamn sentence. Because a sudden arc of energy blasted up from the wreckage of the fallen Cue-tip, an arc of corruscating crapola, connecting with the cloud and exploding in its interior with a massive bang. Instantly coils and transistors rained down, along with a great splash of water that slammed onto the Indians, dousing them thoroughly and plopping them headlong into an instant lake of mud.

"Robots!" said Elliot. "Bill, both those gods were robots! Do you know what that means?"

"Not good! If this means that I'm back on the Planet of the Robot Slaves, then we are in for it."

"We're still in the same place, you idiot. There has got to be an explanation but this is not the time to worry about it! If you want to worry, look over there—keep moving!"

Bill looked. Sure enough, there in the canyon wall was the tunnel entrance. A section of the rock wall was rolling back with a grating, rock-against-metal sound.

"See!" said Bill. "What did I tell you?"

"Well don't just lay collapsed there like a dead bug! We've got to get moving before those Indians recover!"

Bill was thus properly motivated. He scrambled up from the ground and galloped for all he was worth toward the beckoning cave entrance, Elliot thundering along at his side. But the portal was only ajar enough to allow one and a half persons in. Driven on by fear and the urgent sense of survival, the two hit the opening at precisely the same time, wedging themselves into the opening like comedians in a really crappy movie. But there was no polite give-or-take now, no you-first-old-buddy stuff here.

"Troopers first!" shouted Bill, giving Elliot the

elbow as hard as he could.

"No! I'm the Time Cop! I declare this a priority order and insist that I go first!"

After a few moments of intense discussion on the matter, and some desperate shoving, their mutual desire to save their butts drove them into close embrace and popped them through. They stumbled on into the darkened tunnel, Elliot falling flat on his face on a metallic floor and Bill smashing into a bulkhead.

The tunnel door slammed behind them.

Bill immediately smelled the difference. Whereas the outside had been fresh and dry and desertish, sort of smelling like standing in front of a good air conditioner, this dimly lit corridor smelled old, metallic and musty—with just a trace of pizza in the air. In short, it smelled like the infamous old Italian starship Bill had once served on, from the planet Mondo Pizzaiola, the S. S. KAKABENE.

"Wait a moment," said Bill, climbing uncertainly to his feet. "Starship! This place smells like the corridor of a starship!"

"Exactly, Bill," said Elliot, rubbing his nose. "That's why I pointed out the wobbling sun."

"Why should a starship corridor be attached to a desert canyon wall?" asked Bill, thoroughly baffled and buffaloed by the mystery.

"Don't you understand, you ninny? Didn't the fact that those gods were robots mean anything to you? It's because—"

Elliot broke off, horrified, interrupted by a figure coming forward, pushing something long and ominous in front of him. Strangely sinister-looking too, thought Bill, squinting fearfully into the dimness. Some kind of terrible savage weapon? Some grim lesser god to avenge the ones they had knocked off?

No, actually, he could see as the creature came closer. See what hideous artifact it was pushing before it—

A broom.

And pushing the broom was a large brawny man in a khaki jumpsuit. He had thick shoulders and not one but two heads.

It was too late to hide, so Bill just walked over and held out his hand in traditional Phigerinadon greeting to janitors. "Howdy, neighbor."

"Greetings, guys," said the longer-haired head of the two-headed big guy. "What are you strangers doing here? We usually sweep up nothing but bones and skulls hereabouts. Never had ourselves a couple of live people before, have we, Bill?"

"Nope, Bob. We sure haven't. A yup, a yup," mumbled the other head, with short spiky hair and moronically vapid features.

"We're Bill-Bob!" explained the friendly custodian. "We're of the New People!"

"Duh—yeah! We're moo-tated moo-tineers!" drooled the other head.

"Perhaps you mean to say that you are mutated mutineers?" suggested Elliot hopefully.

"No, we worship the Holy Cow, from which all things drip, including intelligence," said Bob. "You've got to excuse my inferior half. He was behind the door when they passed out the brains!"

"Damn, Bob! I was? I wish you would have called me. I always wanted a brain!"

Bill was horrified at this dreadful spectacle before them!

How could someone so stupid possibly be named "Bill"?

And then he had a thought.

"Oh. You must be one of those Bills with only one L," he said.

"Nope!" said the moo-tant. "I'm a Bill that's got THREE Ls!" said Billl proudly.

"No you don't, ninny. You've got two!"

"Two? I want another one! I've been cheated!"

Bill, disgusted with the argumentative mutant, was about to kick the creature where it would do the most good, but Elliot took matters immediately into hand. "This really is absolutely ridiculous. Bill-Bob, or whoever you are—we are agents of Justice. I assume that you can take us to your ship's officers, to whoever is in charge here!"

"Officers? In charge?" Bill glottled, his stupid expression mirroring that of the cretinous Bill facing him.

"Bill, you really are an incredibly ignorant victim of military brain-washing. Hasn't any of this filtered through that great gob of gristle on top of your shoulders? The valley, the wobbly sun, the robots, the two-headed mutated mutineer with the broom—and here's the clincher, the metallic corridor?"

Bill muttered and scratched his head. "This one's a toughie, Elliot. Maybe it turns out that the ancient American West is a much weirder place than anything in the comix, that's for sure!"

"No, you gormless government-issued gob-brain. We're on a *spaceship*. We haven't gone back in time at all! That unreliable Time Portal took us to the wrong place! That hippie didn't come here; he's gone someplace—some time entirely different!"

"Golly," muttered the moronic mutated mouth, "that fellow sure uses long words. What that first word mean? The long one: 'no'?"

Bill pondered the idea and did not understand it at

all. "Come on, Elliot, why would someone put a desert and a valley on a giant spaceship?"

"Why would anyone put *you* on a starship? That's the question I've been asking myself, Bill."

"Look," said Bob. "I hate to interrupt this convivial discussion, but I've got a hell of a lot more sweeping up to do before I get my evening bowl of gruel and cup of milk in reward. Do you want me to take you to the bridge or not?"

Elliot skipped and capered with joy. "You see! You see, Bill, he said *bridge*. So there must be a bridge. And the bridge must be on a spaceship. So this *is* a starship!"

"A bridge could be across a river, too," Bill muttered darkly, still not sure just what the hell was happening.

"I feel that I must warn you though," warned Bob. "The captain's really a bit loony. Gone clear out of his mind, if you ask me. It takes one to know one and I know one not one neck away from me. But we moo-tated moo-tineers, we've learned our lessons. We just do our menial jobs, try to forget the past, go to church on Sunday, no more wanking on the planking—and we keep our noses clean. Which is especially hard when you've got two noses, right Bill?"

"Dat's right, Bob. Whatever you said. It's dem long words again, like 'I' and 'me.' "

"Let's get to it then, huh," Elliot muttered impatiently. "But first . . . is there any chance that we can get a look at that sun? I find it most intriguing—not to say impossible inside a spaceship."

"The sun? Sure thing! The solar footplate engineer, he's a good buddy of mine!"

"What kind of engineer did you say?"

"Ah, come on . . . I'll show you exactly what I mean." The two headed moo-tant gestured.

Bill and Elliot followed the shambling figure down the long, curved corridor. After a long and tiring walk, they reached a door that squeaked open when Bill-Bob grabbed the handle, put his weight upon it and hauled. They all stepped through.

Bill had seen some remarkable not to say interesting things in his life, but this took the brass battleship.

Bill-Bob, Elliot and Bill stood upon a ramshackle metal platform a few feet above a chintzy tinfoil and papier-mache surface that stretched to the horizon. Painted blue, with rust and rivets showing through in places. It didn't make sense. Train tracks stretched out across it. Bill jumped down, walked along the tracks a bit—then looked up.

And dropped, whinnying with terror, fingers clamped to the tracks. For above him was the desert, the rocks, the Indians. And he was falling toward them!

"Falling! This is the end!" he screeched.

"Knock it off, cretin!" Elliot sneered, walking over and standing beside him, bending to pull his clamped fingers loose from the rail. "You're not going to fall—even though you *are* standing on the sky. . . ."

"You think that makes it any better!"

"Look, dummy—am *I* falling? Or our two-headed guide? We're inside a hollow spaceship, that's all. Which is spinning in space so everything is held to the inside by centrifugal force. You *have* heard of centrifugal force, haven't you?"

"Yes—but I forget."

"Educational standards are not what they should be. Look—what happens if you fill a pail of water, tie a rope to it and swing it around your head?"

"I get wet?" Bill said hopefully.

"Yes—*you* probably would. But anyone else would swing it fast enough in a circle so the water wouldn't come out—"

"Thar she blows!" the two-headed janitor shouted.

The sun was coming toward them across the sky-ground, accompanied by a distant tooting. As it came closer the sun grew dimmer and they could see a dilapidated steam engine on the track ahead of it.

"Casey! Casey!" the moo-tant hailed.

"Yo, Bill-Bob! How they hanging?" said the man in the cab of the engine as it approached. He pulled a cord attached to a steam whistle, and the whistle blew like a lost and hopeless soul dropping down through the void into purgatory. Or something like that. Then the engine went through a cloud and they saw the special effects generators that hummed and cranked, projecting cloud images onto the sky, weaving out their webs of cheesy cinematic magic upon the unsuspecting tribes of warped Indians on the desert below.

But the most incredible sight was still the old-fashioned steam-engine train on rusty steel railroad tracks, struggling to drag the weight of a fusion-generated sun across the "sky."

"Wow!" enthused Elliot. "Talk about Apollo and his chariot! This baby has the old myths beat by a mile."

"Wuzzat?" said Bill.

"Never mind. Mythic allusion beyond your education and/or intelligence, Bill."

Still, it was quite a sight, a railroad train hauling a sun across a fake sky. And Bill now could see why the sun had been wobbling so much—the track was clearly old and dilapidated, and if the sun and the train were not tilting and shifting preciously all over the place, the track itself was. Bill, peering down at the sight from his vantage point, got nauseous just observing this twisted parody of nature.

"Astonishing, wouldn't you say, Bill?" Elliot observed. "You see what I mean? That's a whole captive universe down there."

Bill looked dubious. "More like a giant sandbox!"

"That's Casey Moo-Jones, the artificial sun engineer. Casey, these guys say they're time-travelers who've come here by mistake!"

The big, red-faced man spit out a stream of tobacco juice, then bit into a chunk of tobacco and chomped, eyeing the newcomers. "Why'd anyone want to come here, 'cept by mistake?"

"Can you tell us something about how this place got to be like this?" asked Elliot.

"Damned if *I* know. How come I got three thumbs?" The engineer held up his blackened digits in triple illustration.

"Because you're a moo-tation, Casey!" Bob laughed.

"Holy Cow! That's right. Well, 'scuse me guys, but ole Betsy here's acting up again, and I got aways to go before I hit sundown and can turn her off." He pointed over to the edge of the cheap theatrical panorama. "Then I gotta haul this dilapidated old thing around the ridge track and set her up for tomorrow's run. Whew—what a grind!"

"Well, Casey," said Bob, "we all know that you can do it. Haven't missed a day yet, except one or two when you ran out of coal, but we all enjoyed the extra night's sleep. Except the Indians of course. See you."

"I hope so—just as long as the old sun keeps on rolling along! Now you better take these newcomers up and introduce them to the captain. Remember to watch out for the bad moo-tations though, fellows. Well, gotta get moo-ving! Ain't no milk run, I'll tell you that. Har har."

The two—no, three moo-tants laughed at this bovine humor; then Casey Moo-Jones pushed on the creaky mechanical throttle and it ground and hissed steam and chugged forward, dragging its bright, glowing baggage behind it.

"How instructive—no wonder you people mutate!" said Elliot. "That sun looks dangerously radioactive."

"The sun?" Bob waved away the notion. "Naw. You should see the breeder reactor that powers this boat. You could grill an entire herd of cattle on it!"

"Blas-phem-y!" moaned the moo-Bill.

"Oh, that's right," said moo-Bob. "We don't eat hamburgers or steaks or any beef on this vessel, 'cos of the offense given to the Holy Cow, praises be to Her Holy Udders!"

"Religious discussions later," Elliot broke in. "That bridge you mentioned. You'll take us there next, right?"

"Oh yes, no problem."

"But Bob," said moo-Bill. "Uh, you remember what happened last time!"

"Don't worry about it, brother! All you have to do is keep your mouth shut! You think you can go for an hour without saying anything stupid?"

"Duh—can I say something smart?"

"Let's not risk your judgment. Just keep your trap shut, okey doke? We don't want to hear nothing like 'generation ship.'"

"Okey doke!"

The moo-tant clamped his teeth tightly shut.

"What's this captain you've been talking about?" asked Elliot.

"You'll see."

"You think I can use his radio? Maybe I can patch it to communicate with my superiors!" Elliot looked hopeful.

"You're going to have to talk to the captain about that first," said moo-Bob. "Let's go. Hey, brother. This is sure a heck of a lot better than broom duty, huh?"

"Mmmmmmph!" said moo-Bill, unable to say much with his mouth closed.

CHAPTER 12

ON THE WAY DOWN THE MUSTY, DUSTY corridors two things occurred to Bill.

One was that he sure would like a drink.

The other was that he hadn't the faintest idea of what their two-headed guide was talking about. What was a generation ship anyway?

"What's a generation ship?" he asked Elliot as they tagged along behind the happy custodial moo-tant on the way to the fabled bridge. "Is it like maybe a ship's electricity generator?"

"Boy!" said moo-Bob. "This guy's dopier than my brother!"

"Hmmmmmph!" said moo-Bill emphatically.

"No, Bill. *That's* 'generator.' This is 'generation.' You know, like a lot of people descended from each other. Each one's a generation."

"What about it then?" Bill muttered, still unaware.

"I know what a generation is. What's it got to do with a ship?"

"Listen and learn, oh school dropout. Generation ships, well, they're a part of ancient Earth history, while there was still an Earth to have a history about. Which you would have known if you had not cut so many classes."

"Earth. I'm up on that. Inventors of beer, wine and distilled spirits!"

"And home of the Original Holy Cow!" said moo-Bob.

"Well, I suppose we'll hear about that later, won't we?" said Elliot. "But for right now, I think I'd better answer Bill's question. You know, Bill, there weren't always faster than light starship drives, and bloater drives and such. There wasn't even space travel. In fact, as no doubt you can surmise from our experience down in that captive universe of the American Southwest, people used to ride around on horses. Can't get from planet to planet or from star to star very well on a horse, now can you?"

Elliot went on to explain, in boring detail, how when human science believed what Einstein's Theory of Relativity said about matter not being able to travel past the speed of light, yearning hearts and minds nonetheless desired to travel out to settle the stars in their restless urge for progress, conquest, and bigger, better wars. That's when some fascistic moron came up with the ridiculous idea of imprisoning people in a big spaceship and shooting them out toward the stars. Where, just possibly, the surviving remote descendants of the long-dead first crew might reach and settle distant planets.

This highly dubious concept encouraged other scientists to suggest that, the basics of human need thus satisfied, an entire colony could travel through space for the years necessary to arrive at neighboring solar systems. True, it would take many generations of human civilization to arrive at their destination, but with all the comforts of home, how could people refuse? They tried to, not being enamored of being shot off on a one-way trip, but isn't that what MPs and the draft and press gangs are for? Manacled and weeping, the "volunteers" of the first generation ships were dispatched from Earth.

Unfortunately, two factors intruded.

The first was that no sooner had the first batch of generation ships been dispatched, than all the various sorts of FTL drives began to be discovered. Mankind gradually forgot all about these space-faring closed societies traveling to such spots as Alpha, Beta and Proxima Centauri.

The second was that as things got old and fell apart on these ships, they couldn't be fixed or replaced. So civilization aboard most of these ships degenerated to savagery. The highly complex technology was forgotten and the piloting systems went kafluey, driving the whole works off course and into oblivion.

Such was clearly the case with this particular generation ship.

"But what about the captive universe?" asked Bill. "Why would anybody put a desert aboard a starship?"

"Clearly, Bill, because someone had foreseen the possibility of civilization degenerating thusly. Therefore, why not import an artificial civilization modeled on an older self-sufficient people, keep them chained to confining belief systems and then, when they made it to another world, reeducate them? Certainly a concept that might see that at least a couple of ships made it to those distant worlds."

Yes. Bill had to admit that he could definitely see the case for this argument.

"That takes care of the Indians all right," Bill said. "But where do these mutants come from?"

"I have a feeling we are going to find out very soon. You heard the word mutiny. Maybe they took over from the original leaders—mutinied—and started piloting the generation ship."

"But toward where?"

"That's what we're going to have to find out."

"On the bridge?"

"I see you are beginning to think—even though it is still an effort. So we're off to see this captain—and maybe even this Holy Cow . . . the resident deity, it would seem."

As they talked, they had traveled along the musty dusty corridors, dimly lit by grimy 15-watt bulbs, half of them burnt out. Now as they turned to follow another corridor, Bill noticed a porthole through which tiny bright lights peered and twinkled.

"Stars!" said Bill.

"No," said moo-Bill. "That's just the Holy Firefly collection. We tech folk aren't allowed to look at stars. Only the Udderly Holy Cow Monks can gaze upon the bright fury of the stars!"

"They're just these bright lights in space, that's all," shrugged Bill. "No big deal."

"Let's not fumble with sacrilege, Bill," suggested Elliot. "Stars are gods to some people!"

"Gods, shmods!" said moo-Bill. "Da stars dey just big shiny Holy Cow droppings!"

His brother slapped him sharply and immediately

across his forehead. "I told you to keep your mouth shut, dammit!"

The dumber pair of the moo-tant twins looked infinitely chagrined. "Oop!" And he promptly clenched his teeth shut again, putting their mutual hands over his mouth.

The two-headed moo-tant led them on down the hallway, which opened into a large balcony overlooking a large deserted open area with doors and corridors leading from it.

"Hey—what's in there?" asked Bill, pointing toward a bank of refrigerator windows.

"Take a guess," said Bill-Bob.

"Booze!" said Bill, getting excited.

"Mmmmph!" said moo-Bill, looking even more excited than Bill, but refraining from speaking.

Moo-Bob looked very pleased with himself. "No. Guess again?"

"People in suspended animation?" suggested Elliot, honestly puzzled.

"Nope!" said moo-Bob. "Dairy products!"

"Dairy products?" gasped Elliot, aghast.

"Got any fermented yak milk?" queried Bill, quickly sifting through the alcoholic possibilities.

"Nope. Butter, whole milk, skim milk, half and half. Cream, low-fat milk. Cheeses of a delicious array and assortment. Buttermilk, etcetera, etcetera, right brother?"

"MMmmmph!" said moo-Bill.

Bill-Bob started off for the dairy department, but Elliot grabbed him. "You're supposed to be taking us to this infamous bridge of yours to introduce us to your captain!"

"The bridge? The captain?" said moo-Bob, eyes a

little glazed. "Oh yes! Of course! Sorry, I get a little carried away when I get near dairy products of any kind!"

"No yak's milk, huh?" said Bill, disappointed.

Bill-Bob took them to a large round metal portal. He irised it open. He did this by pulling up irises from a nearby flower box and tossing them at the door.

They stepped through onto the generation ship's bridge.

Bill of course had been on many a ship's bridge before, just to polish the brass, even though most of his time he'd spent on laser-cannon fodder detail down in the bowels of the Emperor's behemoth ships prowling space, on the lookout for evil Chingers in order to frustrate their evil ambitions. Or at least that's what it said in the *Trooper's Daily*.

Most of the Emperor's ship's bridges were utilitarian, consisting of a lounge chair with a seat belt for the captain, a lounge chair without a seat belt and a joy stick for the pilot, and plenty of techs who did the real work with lots of buttons, toggles and mindboggles that controlled the hi-tech super-science stardrives. Since the captain and the pilot were upper-class idiots, their controls were not functional at all.

However, this one was quite different.

All of the controls were set into beautiful streamlined rows, glittering with incredible blinking lights, shuddering with breathlessly glorious holographic images of the stars and planets and comets and nebulae beyond. It was the most beautifully sculpted bit of architecture Bill had ever seen, with banks of computers far more futuristic looking than the neo-old-fashioned utilitarian designs utilized by the Emperor's ships.

But the most astonishing sight of all, to Bill, was the captain and the crew.

"Captain Moonure, sir!" said the custodial mutant. Two hands shot up to two brows in salute. "Janitor third-class Bill-Bob reporting! We've got guests, sir. And guess what! They're Time Travelers!"

"Galloping galaxies!" gasped Elliot. "They're cows!"

Yes, observed Bill. They were indeed cows. They were not men with cow heads or cows with human heads. They were not mutated cows or mutated humans. They were just run of the mill, cud-chewing Bessies, staring dully at nothing much, occasionally feeding on hydroponic grass, flicking tails at flies.

"Captain!" said Bill-Bob, walking up to one. "This is Bill and this is Elliot!"

"Moo!" said the captain. "Mooooooo!"

It lifted its tail and did what cows always do when they lift their tails.

"You see!" said moo-Bob. "A real character, the captain, huh? What a joker!"

Just in case, so as not to offend any possible intelligence, Elliot walked up, extending his right hand in the official Galactic handshake. "Greetings, Captain!"

"Moo!" said the cow, and it chewed on some more grass.

Elliot shook his head. "They're just cows!"

"Just cows!" said the mutant janitor. "How can you say that? They're not just cows. They're Holy Cows. Especially bred for godhood and generation-ship piloting!"

Bill nodded, recalling his civilian ambition before he became a Trooper. "Damned fine fertilizer technicians too, from the looks of them!"

Bill-Bob grinned. "Yes! Yes, Bill. I can see that at least you understand!"

"No wonder this ship got off course and lost!" said Elliot. "Even the ancient Hindus were better off. At least they didn't let their sacred cows fly spaceships!"

"Moo," said a cow cleverly. "Moooooooo!"

"Can't you see! You're upsetting them!"

"Look," said Elliot disgustedly. "If you don't mind, could I take a look at your communication equipment? Like I said, somehow I might be able to call up my headquarters."

"You'll have to talk to the communications officer," said moo-Bob, pointing over to a smaller cow by a panel. "Lieutenant Elsie!"

"Moo!" said Lieutenant Elsie.

"Hey! She doesn't seem to mind!" said Bill. "Go to it, Elliot."

Shaking his head, Elliot did so. As he fuddled with the wires and computer, puzzling them out, Bill-Bob brought Bill a glass of milk and cookies, which Bill thought a disgusting substitute for beer but which he drank anyway because he was thirsty, while the cow-crew of space pilots serenaded him with gentle soothing moos.

Bill had to admit that while it was all pretty boring, it was sure a lot better than being barbecued by wild Indians.

"Okay, Bill," said Elliot. "I just hope this works."

Elliot began to tap out the special Time Police S.O.B. (Save Our Butts) call.

Within just a few seconds, help materialized, though not quite in the form expected.

"Greetings, chaps!" said Sir Dudley the Time Portal as he materialized on the generation ship's bridge. "Oh, I say—this is really not done!"

For Sir Dudley had materialized on top of that which, for the sake of purity, might be referred to as the sought-after treasure of the dung-rolling beetle.

"There you are!" shouted Bill. "Now what was the idea of taking us here?"

"Try not to get shirty, dear boy. Even ancient Time Beings are permitted to make tiny *faux pas* from time to time. Is one permitted to ask what all these cows are doing on a ship's bridge?"

"A lot more good than you've been doing us!" said Elliot crossly. "I take it that the hippie from Hell-world isn't here!"

"Uhm, well actually, no. He nipped down to about 1939, in New York City. United States of America. Back on long-since-destroyed Earth before it was destroyed. Don't know how I shipped you boys here, but I intend to make it up. Forthwith, dare I say. And, dear comrade Elliot, to make some amends for my tiny mistake, I have brought along the most up-to-date version of a Time Patrol Control Watch. It is from the far future and is far superior to earlier models. Comes with a twelve-month guarantee and a built-in video game."

"Greatly appreciated," Elliot said as he strapped the gleaming gadget on.

"Just don't hurt any of our cows!" said moo-Bill, looking not a little alarmed at the appearance of the talking Time Portal.

"I don't think you need to worry," said Elliot.

"So, if you would be so kind as to step on through," said Sir Dudley, "I'll shuttle you gentlemen to the exact time and place where the hippie went to change time. I assume that will soothe tempers and make some amend for past follies."

"I suppose it will have to do," muttered Elliot.

Bill took one last gulp of milk and followed Elliot Methadrine through the Time Portal toward Somewhere Else in Time.

"Moo," mooed the Starship Cows and went back to eating grass, chewing cud and producing cow-pats.

"Oh well," said moo-Bob. "Back to work, eh, Bill?"

"Uh . . . yeah, Bob. And then we can go and read our horny porny comix. Isn't that right, Otto?"

A man in a Nazi storm trooper outfit and a riding crop stepped out from the closet where he'd been hiding. "Hmm. Yes. Meantime, it would seem as though I've a little trip to make back in time!"

"Sieg heil!" said the crypto-Nazi cows. "Sieg heil!"

C H A P T E R **13**

"NEW YORK SQUARED, THAT'S WHERE WE are," Elliot said, squinting at the direction indicator map cross-reference dial on his new Time Patrol Control Watch.

"What kind of a dumb name is that?" Bill sneered.

"I have no idea—but that's what it says here. New York, New York. Maybe they like the city so much that they named it twice."

Although Bill was not exactly the cosmopolitan sort, he'd seen his share of cities throughout the Empire. He'd seen cities alien, cities human and cities not quite either. He'd seen small cities—and of course there was Helior, the Galactic Capitol, the planet that was just one big city.

But this city, this New York, New York, was like nothing Bill had ever seen before.

He sort of liked it. Even though it stank.

He didn't like the doggie-do on his shoe, however, which he scraped off on the curb, avoiding other scattered mounds of the same substance. What he did like, however, were the little hats and gray and drab clothes the people wore. Nice and old-fashioned. What he liked even better were the bars on almost every corner. A gleaming contrast to the general blockiness of the place, and most of all the clear surliness of the citizens.

In short, it reminded him of back home on Phigerinadon II, and it made him feel homesick.

Sir Dudley the Time Portal wavered in the air. "Ahh, there you are. Simply wizard to see that you have arrived safely."

Elliot looked up skeptically at the granite building before them. "You sure that this is the place you let that hippie off?" He pulled out his new Time Ticker and consulted the digital readout. "Hmm. Looks okay to me."

"Indeed it should. I do recall that he wanted this particular building, the offices of SUPREME COMICS. ACNE PUBLISHERS. Well, must dash."

"Hey. How do we get back home?"

"Simple," said Sir D. "When you're finished here, you can find me at the 1939 World's Fair in Flushing. I'll be at the British Pavilion, watching a cricket match. You might enjoy the other exhibits as well. Toodle-oo!"

He wavered a bit—then vanished.

"I hope he doesn't get lost there," muttered Bill.

"Keep the faith, baby. Come on Bill. Next stop, the offices of SUPER DUPER COMIX. According to my machine here, the editor is currently Kraft-Nibbling, father of horny-porny comix."

Bill looked down the street. "Isn't that a bar down there? You must be thirsty. Why don't we have a drink first?"

"I can understand your misplaced interest in me. Particularly since my arm is now well healed and I can bend it again to lift a drink. But, if you please Bill, later. Also, if you help me get this mess straightened out, I'll see to it that the Time Police will personally buy you your own bar using the Police Pension Fund."

Bill frowned. "You wouldn't bowb an old buddy?"

"Never! This is an important job you're on, Bill. The fate of the universe rests on our shoulders. A bar seems a small reward."

"How about hiring some lady bartenders for my bar, so I won't have to work too hard?"

"Let's not get too greedy, Bill."

"You're on! One successful mission—one bar." Bill squared his shoulders and marched ahead toward the revolving doors of the office building. He stepped inside and started twirling round and round. He got dizzy and sick. When he came out, he still wasn't inside the building, and he fell on top of Elliot.

"It's some kind of trap!" Bill said. "A trap!"

"No, Bill," said Elliot. "This is an ancient type of portal called revolving doors. When you get to the other side, you step out. You don't keep going around like you just did."

"Oh."

Bill, feeling a little queasy—and more than a little stupid—picked himself up and tried again. He stepped into the revolving doors, but pushed a little too hard. He went around and around, and fell out— this time, fortunately, on the other side.

Elliot came through the revolving doors and circled his lips at Bill's attempts to dust himself off. He shook his head.

"Bill, just don't do that in the editorial offices, okay? We Time Cops have got a certain amount of dignity to maintain."

"That's okay, Elliot," said Bill. "I feel much better now."

"Then let's go find that hippie!"

The elevator disgorged them onto a drab carpet in front of a drab set of offices. A sign on one read, ACNE PUBLISHING.

Bill was quite impressed by the array of comix displayed in the foyer. They were thick things, with beautiful artwork, featuring keen-looking detectives, and slant-eyed oriental villains, bug-eyed monsters and women with bobbed hair and incredible bosoms, slinkily covered—often in slips that rose well up their thighs to reveal lacy panties.

"How do you get them to move and hear the sound effects?" Bill asked.

"You don't. What you see is what you get. This is the distant past—remember. And these are pulps," said Elliot, consulting his Time Ticker. "A popular form of magazine, containing mass-market fiction in the nineteen twenties, thirties and forties. The covers promised a lot—the contents delivered little. If you moved your lips when you read, then this was for you.

"ACNE apparently published quite a few of them—as well as all kinds of cruddy general interest nonfiction magazines. Then Kraft-Nibbling started up their Comix line."

"Huh?" Bill was still looking at the colorful babes on the covers.

"Never mind, Bill. Let's just go in and see Kraft-Nibbling, shall we?"

"Sure." Bill picked up a copy of a pulp called SPICY DEFECTIVES with a particularly alluring blonde on the cover.

At a desk sat a sultry secretary.

"Time Police," said Elliot, flashing his badge. "We're here to see Kraft-Nibbling. Official Transchronic Business."

The brunette blinked and stopped chewing her gum. "I'm sorry. No salesmen allowed."

"And I'd like to meet the model for this painting," said Bill, showing her the copy of SPICY DEFECTIVES.

"The door is right behind you—don't let the handle get you in the butt on the way out."

"These are the offices of SUPER DUPER CO-MIX, are they not?" said Elliot in his best stern and authoritarian voice.

"Beat it, will you buster—"

"Furthermore, this is where the editors work."

"You hard of hearing, Mac?"

"Thank you very much." Without further adieu, and ignoring the angry shrieks behind him, Elliot chuntered into the offices, dragging Bill with him.

They walked into a modest, basic office with filing cabinets, desks and bookshelves. Upon the walls hung framed covers of SUPER DUPER COMIX, showing colorful starships, aliens and gorgeously rendered planets and star formations. In one corner was a tall man with longish, unkempt hair standing beside a refrigerator, industriously scribbling away on a sheaf of papers. He seemed to have finished with one piece of paper; he pulled it off its tablet and deposited it in an empty milk crate, where a huge pile of scribbled-upon papers had already accumulated. The big-boned man seemed totally oblivious to the newcomers.

Not so the other man in the room. The seated man looked up from a neatly arranged desk. He was an older man, with graying, slicked-back hair. He wore a tie and round spectacles. He looked up and scowled.

"How did you jokers get in?"

"Through the door!" Elliot sneered. "You are Kraft-Nibbling—the editor of ASTOUNDING. Don't deny it!"

"William Kraft-Nibbling? Father of the atomic bomb? Hardly," said the owlish-looking man, blinking with surprise. "But I am editor of SADO-MASO SUPERMEN!"

Elliot shook his head as though to clear it. "The father of the atomic bomb—something's wrong here. Who are you?"

"Why, Maxwell Perkins, of course. Remember that name as you leave."

Bill of course had never heard of Perkins; however, Elliot, keen student of history, apparently had. He nonetheless checked his Time Ticker to be certain.

"Maxwell Perkins—famous editor at Scribners. Editor of F. Scott Fitzgerald, Ernest Hemingway and Thomas Wolfe, amongst others?" he said, looking down at the digital readout.

"Yes, you finally got something correct. In fact, that's Thomas Wolfe right over there beside that refrigerator. . . . How's it going, Tom?"

". . . of wandering forever and her breasts again . . . of seed-time, bloom and the mellow-dropping oversexed juveniles. And the flowers, the rich flower genitalia of the countryside. . . ." The gigantic, rumpled author muttered like a man possessed. He finished the page and then dropped it into the milk crate.

"Yes! Sounds quite excellent, Thomas!" Maxwell Perkins looked over at the new arrivals. "It'll need some trimming, of course, for comix continuity. Wolfe does go on. But then, that's what I'm paid for. Tom's writing the new serial for TITILLATIONS—a juicy item titled LINGAM AND YONI ON THE RIVER OF LOVE. In a way it is kind of a sequel to Fitzgerald's GREAT GATSBY'S GREAT ORGAN."

"Wait a minute," said Elliot. "Thomas Wolfe and F. Scott Fitzgerald never wrote horny-porny comix!"

"Well of course they write horny-porny!" said Perkins, indignant. "They are the greatest writers of our time—and horny-porny is the greatest literary innovation of the twentieth century!"

Bill was looking at the covers on display. He read the titles of stories out loud. "THE ERECTION ALSO RISES by Ernest Hemingway. THE SEX-CREATURES FROM THE SOUTH by William Faulkner. Wow! Sounds like great stuff."

"Something's wrong," said Elliot, shaking his head morosely. "Something's definitely wrong! Either Sir Dudley put us in an alternate universe. Or that hippie went back much further in time!"

Bill was tapping on a framed cover. "I don't suppose you'd have a comix adaptation of THE PREVERTS OF MAGIC MOUNTAIN STRIKE BACK by Thomas Mann, would you? That looks like a really hot story!"

"Incredible stylistic advances!" said Perkins. "Art and sex bound together. And does it sell!"

"Wait a minute . . . you say that Kraft-Nibbling invented the atomic bomb?"

"That's right."

"But it's not supposed to be this way . . . there's been a terrible mistake." He noticed a newspaper clipping on the desk, picked it up, and read the headline. "COMMUNIST TRAITORS EXECUTED FOR STEALING NUCLEAR SECRETS FOR RUSSIANS. What's all this—fiction?"

"Nope—hard fact," said Perkins. "The Chief of the S.S. caught them red-handed!"

"S.S.!" said Elliot. "You mean to tell me that the United States is run by a Nazi government?"

"Please, we don't use that term anymore since Uncle Adolph changed it in 1936. It's now the 'National Capitalists.'"

"The Nakies?" said Bill.

"How astute. Some say it's a shame about the colored people, but boy, my train from Connecticut sure gets to the station on time now!"

Grasping for understanding, Elliot turned to Perkins. "But you say that Kraft-Nibbling invented the nuclear bomb—and wait a minute—Thomas Wolfe is supposed to be dead now. . . ."

The large, gangling writer suddenly took notice. "Horny-porny comix saved my life!" he said with total conviction. "Why, when I first read 'THE SEXUAL ADVENTURES OF HUCKLEBERRY FINN,' by Mark Twain, I knew I'd found my mode of expression!"

"I don't understand," said Elliot, totally baffled.

"A Fascist American government? Publishing dominated by horny-porny! We're going to have to go
and consult with Dudley again. We've got bigger
problems here than I thought possible! Come on,
Bill!"

CHAPTER **14**

THEY STOOD AT A BUSY CITY INTERSEC-
tion. Elliot was consulting his Time Ticker.

"Queens," he said. "That's where Sir Dudley said
he was going. It is a portion of New York City where
they are having a fair or carnival of some kind. Looks
like we have to take a subway to get there."

"What on Earth—or under the Earth—is a subway?" asked Bill.

"What I mean, of course, is a subway 'train,' Bill.
And, according to the directions displayed on this
machine, we should take the 'N' train, and there is
an entrance right up here at the corner."

"Why can't we take a sky cab?" complained Bill,
not enamored of underground journeys in ancient
apparatus.

"Because right now we are back in time way before
sky cabs, Bill. And I don't have enough local currency

to take a regular cab. According to the Ticker, the subway only costs a nickel—which is five of the cents here—and I found this twenty-five cent piece on the ground. Understand any of this higher mathematics?"

Bill grunted monosyllabically. In truth he had not been paying attention to the sums but had been admiring the sign, BAR, on a building ahead.

"How about a beer?" he suggested.

"No money, no time. Down here." Elliot led him down a set of cement steps toward the dim and subterranean world of New York transportation.

They did not notice the figure in the gray trench coat, brim of hat tilted low, hands shoved in pockets, black armband labeled 'SS,' furtively following them.

The subway train was an ancient and stinking piece of machinery that swayed back and forth most noisily. Bill began to feel more than a trifle ill. To take his mind off his stomach, he settled down on his seat and examined the line of advertisements running along the top of the car.

"Uncle Adolf loves you!"

"Smoke 'Panzer Strike' Cigarettes!"

"Buy German-American!"

"Drink Bavarian Beer—Or Else!"

The subway train rolled through Queens. All of the passengers got off at stations along the line, except for Bill, Elliot and the guy wearing the trench coat and the hat sitting way down on the other side of the car.

The car wrenched onward, lights sputtering. The contents of Bill's digestive system gurgled sympathetically. Elliot the Time Cop didn't seem to be bothered by the motion and was lost in his Time

Ticker, his face wearing a totally baffled expression. "It just doesn't follow," he murmured, shaking his head mournfully. "Effects indicate a cause... but I can't follow this back along the Time Flow."

All of which set Bill's mind onto what for him might be considered a decidedly philosophical bent. Things seemed so bleak, so depressing, here in this subway car rattling through New York City in a Nazi America of 1939. Which was bad. What was worse was that in addition to being nauseous, he was getting hungry because he hadn't eaten in a long time. He felt black despair descending upon him.

Now, most of the time, this wasn't a problem. Trooper food was usually so full of ego-dissolving chemicals—and the Military Muzak that piped through the official speakers so filled with stress- and identity-reducing subliminals—that Troopers not directly being ripped to pieces in action against the Chingers were usually so doped and droned out they seldom had self-examination difficulties and seldom fell into depression or despair. In fact, the number of Trooper corpses with smiles on their faces since the advent of this Psycho-Cram program was quite phenomenal.

Any other problems were usually self-medicated with alcohol—as Bill had learned so efficiently.

However, if a Trooper did have problems of a psychological nature, all he had to do was to go to the Service Chaplain or Shrink who would let some blood, give a neuro-massage or tap, or, if all else failed, simply do a Brainectomy, which was actually the most efficient method for dealing with emotional and psychological problems, although radical even for the Troopers. However the standard treatment was for a psycho-technician to place two credits in the victim's palm and tell him to go buy a drink on the Emperor.

However, Bill had been gone long enough that he now felt a bit of a psychological withdrawal from all the psycho-soothing he'd received as a servant of Empire. So, now, belly growling and complaining, in a dirty metal coffin rolling underground to the heart of Queens, he began to experience a truly twentieth-century type of angst.

What was the Meaning of Life, anyway? Bill thought, his mind wrenching with self-doubt and his lower extremities rumbling counterpoint.

Suddenly, Bill was filled with sadness.

Oh, how he missed Phigerinadon II.

Oh, how he missed his Mom! Though he couldn't remember her at all.

And most of all, how he missed his robo-mule!

Abdominal distress momentarily forgotten, Bill began to sing the Phigerinadon farm boy's lullaby to his robo-mule.

Bill didn't exactly know what the words meant, but it had a sweet melody and so he'd sung it to his robo-mule every day after working in the field before he oiled him and put him in the shed. The robo-mule—whose name was Ned—seemed to enjoy it and he never once broke down.

A sad and self-indulgent tear dribbled down Bill's cheek. "I miss you, Ned," he moaned. "I really miss you, big guy!"

"Have you gone out of your mind?" Elliot asked. "What's wrong with you?"

Bill knuckled his eye and swallowed. "Something in my eye, maybe."

"I'm not surprised. This is a particularly filthy form of transportation."

Just then, Bill became aware that the man in the trench coat at the far end of the car had moved up and was now standing in front of them, looking dark, sinister and dangerous.

"Here," the man said, handing Bill a handkerchief. "I zee you got something in der eye."

"Thanks," said Bill. He took the hanky and dabbed at his eyes. "Thanks."

"*Bitte schoen.*" The man looked around to see if they were being watched. He then produced a nasty-looking Luger. "How you like mine little *schusser*? His name is Otto. Otto says, you vill tell me who you are and vere you are from!"

"Bill . . ." said Elliot. "It's a Nazi!"

Elliot, showing sudden wild courage, grabbed for the man in the trench coat—but the Luger barked three times before he could reach him. One bullet smashed the Time Ticker, another went through Elliot's neck and the last one went straight through his heart in an bright flower-explosion of blood.

Elliot gurgled, then keeled over onto the subway floor.

Bill looked down at the dead man. He was alone now in a Nazi 1939 New York subway train with a Luger pointed at his head. Bill thought to himself that he'd probably been in worse fixes before, but he couldn't quite remember one right off the top of his head.

"Now perhaps you vill tell me who you are und vere you are vrom," said the Nazi Secret Policeman, for that is surely what he must have been.

"Speak, *schweinhund*. Now tell me. Vot is your name? Wilhelm?"

"Bill. With two Ls."

"*Ja.* You are a member of der Time Police?"

"No. That was my friend Elliot. Me, I'm just a harmless Galactic Trooper. Really I'm out of my jurisdiction here, and I'm not supposed to kill Nazis, I'm supposed to kill Chingers. So you're safe."

The Nazi agent chuckled. "I am relieved. Now, you vill tell me about your dead Time Police friend *und* how you got from the future. *Und* maybe along the vay, you vill give me some stock market information, *ja?*"

"Stock . . . No, Mr. Nazi. You don't understand. I'm from the far, far future. I don't even know what a stock market is. There aren't many markets of any kind any more since the Emperor pretty much owns everything."

"Very interesting. Now . . . you vill tell me the truth! Vy are you spying on us? Vat vere you doing talking to Max Perkins, vere are you going . . . und ven vill der Berlin Panzerblitzen baseball team finally vin der Vurld Series?"

"I—I don't really know!" said Bill. "I mean . . . Elliot and I . . . we're just trying to stop the history of the world from being changed, that's all. You see, Nazis aren't supposed to be in control of things back here. There's something terribly wrong. So if you'll just give me that gun and come along quietly—"

"Der information!" said the Time Nazi. "I vant der info!"

Bill could see that he was in a bit of a serious jam. But wasn't he a Trooper? Hadn't he been trained for combat? Why couldn't he remember what he had been taught? What was the hold you applied to a wrist of the hand holding a gun? He stood slowly and backed away from the menacing Nazi who pushed the gun forward.

Bill stepped back again—stepped into the pool of

blood. And slipped. His foot came up as he fell and kicked the gun from his attacker's hand.

The Nazi agent screamed and floundered backwards.

Bill, seeing his chance, leaped on the man.

The two fell onto the subway floor, flopping and flapping about like a pair of landed fish as they fought over the Luger, which the agent grabbed up again.

"*Schweinhund!*" cried the Nazi agent. "You will die, I say! Die!"

Bill said nothing, too involved in keeping the gun from pointing to his stomach.

The Nazi, recovered somewhat, and with a sudden burst of effort, managed to hurl Bill from him. He stood up, gasping in air and pointed the nasty, thin gun down at Bill where he lay on the subway floor.

"I do not care what mine superiors say! No vun attacks me and survives! You vill die!"

The Nazi's hat had come off in the struggle and Bill could see that his hair was blonde and his straight Aryan features were twisted in a cruel smile.

Even crueler blue eyes flashed as the Nazi aimed the Luger at Bill.

"Heh heh heh!" said the Nazi.

Bill tensed himself for one last lunge before the gun fired.

However, even as the Nazi was pulling the trigger, a sudden ray beam sizzled from nowhere, blasting the man's head clean off his shoulders.

The headless body dropped beside Bill, who scrambled to his feet and looked around for his benefactor.

He saw no one.

He was alone with the two dead bodies as the train hurtled through the subterranean night.

Bill gaped uncomprehendingly. Now what, he

wondered, did this mean? But before he had the opportunity to wonder long, a tiny voice piped from just beyond the body of Elliot!

"Gee Bill," it said. "That was kind of a close call."

CHAPTER 15

"EAGER BEAGER!" GURGLED BILL, WITH no small amount of incredulity.

"Gee, Bill! That's me! But could you exercise some element of intelligence and try to remember to call me Bgr? That's my real Chinger name and I'm mighty proud of it."

Bill looked around. "Where are you?"

"Down here!"

Bill looked down. The voice was coming from the prostrate, shot-up, dead body of Elliot Methadrine! Sure enough, even as Bill watched, his old adversary jumped from the corpse's chest up onto a subway seat. He blew smoke from the muzzle of his tiny blaster, with which he had just separated Nazi head and Nazi hat from Nazi trench coat and, most importantly, Nazi Luger.

Bgr, first known to Bill as "Eager Beager" back

in Camp Leon Trotsky where he did a fantastic job of shining boots, was exactly seven inches tall with four arms, an ugly face and a defensive attitude. Which wasn't surprising since the ambition of the Emperor and all of his fighting forces was to blast every peace-loving Chinger out of existence. Bill's surprise upped a notch as he turned to see that the top of Elliot's head was opening on a hinge, to reveal the compartment that took the place of the brain. There was even a tiny water-cooler in there next to an even tinier porta-potty.

"Control room . . . robot," Bill muttered. "But what about all the blood?"

"Your brain has been damaged by the military and the booze, Bill. Don't you know ketchup when you see it? I had three gallons in the pseudo-flesh of this robot. Nice and gory when needed."

Bill realized then that Elliot Methadrine had been Bgr in metal/flesh disguise all along! Elliot Methadrine had been a sorta-cyborg operated by the enemy. Wouldn't J. Edgar Insufledor be shocked to hear this! Bill wasn't shocked though. He had been around the Chingers far too long.

But even though this was the enemy, Bill was surprisingly cheered to see the little guy.

"Good to see you, Bgr. I know you're the enemy and all that, but at least you have a familiar face. It's no fun being stuck alone on a 1939 subway train going to Flushing, Queens, to the World's Fair to try to find that time portal guy."

"I know, I know," said Bgr. "I'm up on the continuity! Where do you think I've been all this time! I've been Elliot Methadrine!"

"Oh. Yeah. That's right."

"Sometimes, Bill, it's my most fervent prayer to

the Great Chinger in the Sky-Hive that you somehow be made Admiral of the Imperial Fleet. Though on second thought our records reveal that he is even stupider than you."

"Well, thanks Bgr!" said Bill, brightening. "That's probably one of the nicest things you ever said to me. Probably the only nice thing you ever said to me. So what are we going to do now?"

"Gee—I guess first thing we should do, Bill, is to get off at the Flushing stop of this subway train."

"That sounds good to me."

"Glad to see you are finally with it. And then we go and find Sir Dudley the time portal at the cricket match, whatever that is, at something called the British pavilion. And then, pardon the expression, we try and find out what the hell has happened! Everything is apparently all askew! As a keen student of your past history I cannot imagine what could possibly have occurred to allow the Nazis to take over America. I have the strong suspicion that there is a tributary of time that got really bent, to replace mainstream fiction with horny-porny; that has something to do with it."

"Right!" Bill agreed loudly, although he had very little idea of what Bgr was talking about.

"And most importantly," said Bgr, twitching his muzzle rapidly, "we have to assure that the Chingers exist in this crummy universe. Let's go."

Bill got off the subway train at the Flushing stop, allowing the car with the dead Nazi to rumble off into the wilds of Queens. He had Bgr in his pocket, which was most uncomfortable since the Chinger planet was a high-gee planet, and the little alien was no lightweight. Bill stumped his way up the steps and on into the 1939 World's Fair.

"Gee," said Bgr, looking around from his perch in Bill's pocket. "This doesn't look much like the Time Ticker said the 1939 World's Fair is supposed to look—but then, this is a different 1939, isn't it?"

"Yeah. I guess so."

It looked pretty good to Bill. Lots of buildings and rides and concession stands, edibles and drinkables.

"I wonder if there are any bars here?" he queried plaintively.

"Don't even think about booze for a while. We are on a mission."

They moved through the arches into the fair-grounds.

"Those swastikas," said Bgr, pointing at the gigantic bent-cross emblems hanging from the arch and from virtually every building and booth. "I don't believe they're supposed to be there."

"No?"

"Let's just hope that Sir Dudley didn't get into trouble . . . and let's just hope that the British Empire still exists so they have a pavilion here. Gee—it doesn't look too good, Bill. It doesn't look good at all. And I'd hate to be stuck in this particular time!"

Bill was looking at the Oktoberfest displays and the huge number and variety of kegs of beer. Also, it looked as though there was no lack of bars here in 1939. He was a good worker and could probably get a job somewhere. Maybe Bgr didn't like it, but it had the feel of his kind of place.

Still, he was a Trooper.

He had an Emperor to serve.

He had a job to do, an oath to uphold, a loyalty to remember.

Even Bill couldn't actually totally buy this, but he

continued on his mission nonetheless. If for no other reason than that he had been militarily brainwashed and had about as much free will left as a flea.

And Bill liked fairs. He liked them a lot. They would have fairs back on Phigerinadon II, and once, when he was ten years old, his Mom had taken him to the Phigerinadon II World's Fair. It wasn't as big as this 1939 Fair on Earth of course, but to a ten-year-old it was the biggest, most wonderful experience imaginable.

It was at the Phigerinadon II World's Fair that Bill had decided he wanted to grow up to be a Fertilizer Technician. The theme of that particular fair had, in fact, been Better Living Through Fertilizer. Bill, who'd already been working in the fields for five years, marveled at the wonderful new technology and the exciting new strains of fertilizer! Bill had never realized how many different kinds of fertilizers there were and how, through genetic engineering, scientific Mix-mastering and a good, well-trained nose, one could develop just the right fertilizer for just the right crop.

It had been a revelation. The boy had been fascinated. He took the Fertilizer Falls ride over and over again. He performed astoundingly well at the Fertilizer IQ Test.

The Fertilizer Technicians exclaimed with joy at the results, and proclaimed that he was a genius. They wanted to send him off to P.U. on Fertilizer World, awarded with the special Thomas D. Crapper Scholarship.

However, Mom needed him to work the fields, so he couldn't go. Still, those were golden memories at the Phigerinadon II Fair.

And now, here he was at another World's Fair. Bill

could not help but feel a little thrill of nostalgia.

Already he was planning on how to get himself a beer despite Bgr's objections. But he was doing all the walking now so he would tough it out.

So Bill just said, "I'm going to have a beer, Bgr. I don't care what you say."

"I suppose there is no breaking the addiction. But make it fast. And just don't spill it on me, got that?"

Bill fished a dollar bill out of his pocket. Fortunately, the Chinger had foreseen the need for cash here, and before they'd left the subway car they had gone through the dead Nazi's pockets.

The dollar bill portrayed a man named George Von Washington who had a funny-looking black haircut and a postage-stamp-sized mustache.

Bill hurried up to a booth and was soon snozzling into a large stein of beer. Damned good beer, too.

"There," said Bgr. "You've had your fill of your disgusting beverage and habit. Now can we get back to the business of saving our universe?"

Bill, his nerves calmed considerably, nodded. "Yeah, sure. But I've been meaning to ask you, Bgr. Why are you doing this? Why did you masquerade as Elliot Methadrine? And a Time Cop? And also, how come you're on my side?"

"Bill, don't you think that we Chingers foresaw Bad Things with that Time Hole business? There aren't any such things as Time Cops . . . that was just so I could be the boss. And finally—look, as much as Chingers hate your Emperor and your race in general, this kind of time crime must be stopped. It strains the whole time fabric of the universe which, take it from me, is not a good thing."

Bill, generally ignorant of anything outside the military, or fertilizer, which at many times is very much the same thing, hadn't the slightest idea of what Bgr was talking about. But he nodded like a fool and enjoyed the pleasing sensation of his belly full of beer.

Bgr the Chinger directed him to a World's Fair guide and directory.

Bill examined the guide, reading the contents.

Beer Exhibition.

Pretzel Exhibition.

Jackboot Exhibition.

Fun Mit Der Fuhrer.

Schnaps Exhibition.

Wienerschnitzel und Dachshund Exhibition.

Foreign Pavilions of Inferior Races.

"That's it!" said Bgr. "Let's move."

"The Schnaps Exhibition looks good. I even know what that word means. We could start there—"

"Shut up," Bgr smiled. "Saving the fabric of the universe comes first." He popped his head out of the pocket for a quick look. "Come on, this way. According to the directory map, it's right down this row, here."

Bill shrugged and allowed himself to be directed to the British Pavilion.

The British Empire appeared to be in trouble, for the pavilion turned out to be a particularly ramshackle affair, poorly constructed of tea chests and plywood awkwardly tacked together. There were no photos, no samples or demonstrations. Just a rather tattered Union Jack, with a swastika in one corner, nailed to the wall. But a row of dilapidated chairs did face a projection booth where a grainy image of a slothful cricket match was being shown. Before it slumped Sir Dudley—sound asleep.

"Dudley!" said Bgr, head popped out again.

"Indubitably," he responded instantly awake. "But

whom, might I ask, are you?"

"I used to be Elliot."

"I say—you certainly have shrunk!"

"Yes, well, we'll get into that later. Right now, you've got to take us to the place in time where we can stop this madness!"

"Rather! A nasty bit of work, this world, so I wouldn't be adverse to that. But where is the time nexus of the trouble?"

"According to my calculations," said Bgr, "the change that caused this particular Time Line could only have been brought about because all the Bloomsbury group decided to write horny-porny, thus making it a respectable form of literature. Take us to England at the turn of the century, Dudley. To London and Bloomsbury, to the residence of Virginia Wolfe! We need to discuss this business with her!"

"Ahh, dear old Blighty, my pleasure indeed. Just pop inside, if you please."

"That's it, Bill!" commanded Bgr. "Step."

Bill took a firm step forward into the maw of the Time Portal. He was getting to be an old hand at this!

"I say—not quite ready yet!"

Bill tried to stop stepping, but he'd already tripped over the edge.

Bill fell screaming into the Time hole.

The only other sound he heard was Bgr's angry cry as he fell from Bill's shirt pocket.

CHAPTER 16

BILL FELL.

Being a borderline alcoholic, Bill had of course fallen before. But never quite like this. Sometimes he felt like he was falling up, sometimes he felt like he was falling down. Sometimes it felt like he was falling north, south, west and east and all the various combinations, blown by the wildest winds imaginable across skies filled with clouds and unimaginable colors. Skirling music and swirling smells enveloped him. He heard music and voices dopplering all around him, as though he were inside some gigantic radio and some idiot was twirling the channel selector crazily across the wave-band selector.

Bill fell for a long time.

He lost consciousness several times, although he didn't realize it, since the rules didn't seem to work the same here.

Colors, colors, colors.

Music, music, music.

Voices, voices, voices.

Voice: "You there, I see you and I am talking to you."

Bill looked around and saw no one else, so he realized that the voice must be talking to him. He also realized that he was no longer falling. And was sitting in some sort of cloud bank.

"Me?" said Bill.

"You see anyone else I might be talking to?" snapped the voice. "What are you doing here?"

"Well, there was this Time Portal and Bgr the Chinger said that we were supposed to go back to talk to somebody or something. And then—"

"Never mind. That's enough to let me know that things are in their usual mess around you." The voice had a booming, numinous quality—like an admiral on the P.A. system in a starship with reverb. For some reason it made Bill shiver. He looked around him worriedly.

As far as he could see, clouds stretched away in all directions. In the distance, between cracks in the clouds, Bill could see stars. From a break in the clouds above, a single shaft of light shone down like a pillar of fire.

Bill did not like this, was more than a little worried. "Would you, sir, let me know where I am—"

"Shut up!" the voice commanded. "I am going to tell you a joke, Bill, a joke that might give you a clue. Here's the joke." The light quivered mysteriously. "What does an agnostic dyslexic insomniac do?"

"Uhmmm—that's a tough one," he muttered.

"Try harder, Bill. Put some of your so-called brain into it."

"Maybe he doesn't do anything?"

"What a true idiot you are. You're supposed to say, 'I don't know.'"

There was a heavy bass on the voice. The clouds rumbled and quivered, and Bill rumbled and quivered right along with them. The situation was getting more than a little worrying.

"I don't know," Bill finally quavered.

"That's better. Now I deliver the punch line!"

Bill flinched, expecting a fist to appear from nowhere. Stranger things had happened.

"An agnostic dyslexic insomniac stays up all night, wondering if there's a dog!"

The clouds thundered with laughter.

Bill didn't get it, but he figured he'd better laugh too.

"Pretty funny, huh, Bill?"

"You bet, wow, a real yak!"

"I wish I'd made that joke up myself, Bill, I tell you. But I told you that joke for a reason. I generally don't make appearances before people, so when I do I at least try to be slightly oblique about it."

"Oh . . . yeah. I get it," he said, not getting it at all.

"Bill, don't you understand?" rumbled the voice, groaning with exasperation. "There *is* a dog!"

"I never had a dog," said Bill. "I had a robo-mule, though!"

"This borders on the believable. I bet that you can't walk and talk at the same time. Do I have to spell it out for you? Do I have to burn a bush or knock you on the head with tablets or—wait a minute. I know. . . ."

Bill was hardly listening. He was really thirsty and sure could use a drink. And he still hadn't the slightest idea what the invisible voice was talking about. A beer—a really frosty large mug of beer obsessed him.

Zoroaster, he certainly could use one of those!

Suddenly, with a slight pinging sound, a mug of beer materialized before him, just as he'd imagined it!

Bill's reflexes went into gear before his thoughts could engage. He reached out, grabbed the beer and had sucked it halfway down before he realized the miraculous quality of what had just occurred.

"That's pretty good—how is it done?"

The voice seemed fairly writhing with frustration: "That is not the point, you moron. Think about it, my boy. If you can. Think of your previous, unspoken thought. Whose name did you take in vain, wishing for that beer?"

Bill blinked. "Oh. Zoroaster, I think." He continued drinking the beer. And then it hit him.

He spit out a spume of beer.

"Zoroaster! Is that you? I mean I'm sorry, sir— that is I mean—gulp—is that really *you* out there?— you really *exist!*"

"Finally caught on, Bill. This is your god speaking—because you've been a rather bad boy, haven't you? Drinking and chasing girls—and catching them!—and killing Chingers and fragging officers . . . all the things quite against the way you were brought up in your church. Am I wrong?"

Bill's insides turned to jelly. Old childhood terrors and tales of hellfire suddenly spasmed up to the surface of his mind and festered there. He hadn't thought about Zoroaster for a long, long time he realized— he'd backslid! Of course there were chapels and stuff in the service, but they were there only to reinforce the concept of the Emperor as God Incarnate and to spike the communion wafers with training-reinforcement drugs. As a child, Bill had been a model altarboy sort, the pride of his Mother and the lead soprano in the children's choir.

"I haven't been a good Zoroastrian," moaned Bill, head bowed penitently.

"And what happens to my downsliding children?" said the Voice.

"They are chained to a rock in a sea of fire for a thousand years."

"Bill, I'm reaching for the chains." There was a hideous metallic rattling and Bill's stomach dropped into his boots.

"Don't say it, no! You mean . . . you mean I'm *dead*?" With a hideous groan he dropped to his knees, bringing his hands up into contrite prayer. Unfortunately he forgot that he had a half-full mug of beer in his hands and drenched himself.

The Voice tsk-tsked. "Now that's a waste of good beer, Bill."

"Please! Please! A second chance—that's all I want. Let me live and I promise to live a better life, far far better than I lived before!"

"That certainly would not be hard. But actually, Bill, you're not quite dead yet."

"I'm not?"

"No. In fact, you're a pretty healthy guy. You've got to be to take the kind of punishment you've been giving yourself. I see cirrhosis eventually, definitely, but another mortal's liver would have been deep-fried by now!"

"I'm alive!" Bill said, laughing, and dancing around. Suddenly, though, he stopped. "But if I'm not dead—where am I, then?"

"It's a little difficult to explain, Bill, particularly to someone with your attention span. Did you ever push the 'Pause' button on a Holo-VCR?"

"Sure. I have a good technical background."

"You certainly do if you could master something that intricate." There was an edge of sarcasm to the disembodied voice. "Let's just say that's what I did, Bill. Let's just say that I wanted to have a word or two with you."

Bill nodded contritely. "I can understand that, oh mighty in your wisdom and kindness, great Zoroaster. I'm listening. Real carefully. You want me to stop drinking? I'll stop drinking. You want me to stop cursing? I'll stop saying 'bowb' forever. I'll start going to chapel again. But no rock! No chains!"

"Not to fear—that's not my bag. It's a scam some priests dreamed up to keep the peasants in line. Just a myth, actually, Bill. Anyway, I'm not here to threaten you. I thought you'd be interested in an opportunity for salvation, redemption, and double-value for your eternal prayer collection."

Bill nodded eagerly. "Anything you say, Mr. Z."

"I pulled you out of a major goof-up, while you were diving back through the Stuff between Time and Space, so you were pretty accessible. I don't usually take too much notice of mortal affairs, but this business you're involved in is pretty important. So I grabbed the chance to have a word or two with you."

"My pleasure, oh mighty Zoroaster!"

"That's more like it, Bill. A little obsequiousness and writhing goes a long way to cheer a god. I consider myself a pretty lenient deity, as deities go. None of my buddy Jawah's stuff about being vengeful and remorseless—or Allah chopping off hands and so forth. My philosophy toward all universal creation has been pretty hands-off. Free will. Stuff like that. The mess that humanity has gotten itself into is pretty much its own fault. Right?"

"Right, bang-on, sir."

"War, murder, officers, infanticide—they're kind of hard to ignore. But I do my best."

"But killing Chingers, that's great, right, sir? I'll kill lots of Chingers for you! I'll even blast Bgr, if you want!"

"Well, actually, Bill, that's not quite what I had in mind. Particularly since Chingers are actually a lot better creatures than you human beings. Sometimes I think I dropped your prototypes on their heads or something. No, Bill, not Chingers!"

"Horny-porny comix. They'll have to go."

"Not if I have my way. Good fun. I'll miss reading them—but you are close. I suppose they are for the knackers, though. My thanks, my boy, for pointing this out. Perhaps you're smarter than I thought. No, it's certainly not horny-porny, Bill. It's the Nazis."

"The Nazis."

"Yep. The Nazis. Talk about excrescences. They've got to be stopped, or they'll take over the Universe! I feel them breathing down my neck already."

"But—"

"Good question, Bill. Why should they bother Me? Well, I'll tell you. The whole thing is really My fault. If a god could feel guilt, I would even feel guilty. You see, I was cooking up a stew of morals and clean living for a new world I'm designing and I left it in the sun and it turned sour. Not thinking, I just threw it away. Unhappily this mass of decay hit Earth, a country in particular called Germany, and that was it. Need I say more?"

Bill blinked. "So what happened?"

There was a celestial sigh. "Well, obviously I do have to say more. Must I explain everything to you? Obviously, yes. The rot spread, and *voila*. Nazis. Imagine! Nazis, even a lower form of life than lawyers, Emperors or Second Lieutenants."

"So what do I do, Zoroaster?"

"Simple. Fight Nazism. According to my classified sources, they're the ones behind all this Time Slip business. Stamp them out, Bill, you've got my permission and instructions, do that and my light will shine on you!"

"I'll do it, great Zoroaster! All my Trooper training will be put to the test. But I'll do this. But it would help with the transport problem, if you could tell me where they are, get me in touch with the Nazis."

"Well, Bill, as much as I would like to, and I really and truly would, there's the problem of intelligence here. I hate to admit it but I really *don't* know exactly what's going on! Some other deity seems to have a hold on this particular thread of your life, and by golly if he's not doing some fancy cross-stitching with you—"

"But—but—" Bill butted fairly incoherently.

"I know, Bill, it hurts to hear that. I may be immortal but I'm not omnipotent. So you're on your own—although my best wishes go with you of course. So—go get them, tiger!"

And then the clouds parted beneath Bill's feet and he fell once more into total confusion.

CHAPTER 17

TOTAL CONFUSION, PILGRIMWORLD, WAS
a little two-rocket ship town just this side of Nowhere
and well to the Galactic South of Somewhere. It was
a well-known place for colonists to stop off to wet
their feet in the sort of trials and tribulations they
could expect on their respective chosen colony
worlds, and maybe wet their whistles on some of the
famous homegrown moonshine. The theory was, if
you could survive Pilgrimworld's 'shine, you could
weather various and sundry conditions on whatever
hunk of wasted intergalactic rock you'd cast your lot
with.

Bill found himself in the midst of the air, above a
sidewalk here in Total Confusion, dropped, as it
were, from the very fluff of Time. It was a cement
sidewalk, real hard, and Bill had erupted into existence about six feet above it. He went down and hit

hard but—experienced Trooper that he was—turned the fall into a shoulder roll that canceled out most of the impact. He climbed to his feet and brushed himself off. Cursing under his breath, he looked around. Not much of a place.

The sky was green.

In the green sky were two—no, three suns.

A few of the passersby, he noted, were not human. Indeed, they completely ignored him and acted as though Galactic Troopers falling from the sky were an everyday occurrence.

Gigantic flowers grew from the conical tops of buildings. A sweet and sour musk, like hair oil and vinegar, was in the air. In the distance, a rocket landed on a pillar of flame.

"Hmm," said Bill. "I wonder what part of Earth's history I'm in now." He glanced around. "A weird part, *that's* for sure!"

Walking down the road was an old man. Bill called out to him. "Say, Pops—you couldn't tell what era of Earth's history is this?"

"You drunk or something, sonny?"

"No—but I wish I was. It's a simple question, isn't it?"

"Nope. Because this ain't Earth, sonny." The old man spit out tobacco juice. It was a big target but he managed to miss the street and got Bill's boot instead. "This here is Total Confusion!"

"Story of my life," Bill muttered, looking at the brown stain.

"But wherever you go, sonny-boy, you won't be on Earth. Because this here's Pilgrimworld. The Year of Our Heinous Emperor, Stardate 234152!"

Bill blinked. "Why, that's about a year before I

was born. But this is totally another part of the galaxy from Phigerinadon II."

"You talk like you've lost your marbles. War wound?"

Bill scratched his head. Why, he'd been catapulted through space and time to a completely new place. But why? It just didn't make any sense! But then, what in life of late really did? Except, of course, one steady reliable Reality.

"War wound, something like that," said Bill. "One more question—a real easy one. Is there a bar around here?"

"Yep. Reckon so. Just 'round the corner, on Utter Nihilism Street, we got a real nice establishment, name of Sally's Saloon. Tell 'em Willie-Boy sent you!"

"Thanks, Willie-Boy!" said Bill, waving to the old geezer as he hobbled over toward the Saloon.

"Hell, *I* ain't Willie-Boy!" the old man snapped as he staggered away.

But Bill didn't hear him. Visions of beer bottles danced in his head.

Bill rounded the corner marked "Utter Nihilism" and immediately saw the tell-tale neon sign crying out SALLY'S SALOON. He needed a couple drinks before he found out how to get back to Barworld, save the universe from the hippies from Hellworld and the Nazi menace and that kind of thing. He walked into the saloon, which was his kind of bar— dark, damp, smelling of stale beer and dead butts. He grabbed a stool directly in front of a bored-looking bartender with arms the size of Aldebaran hams.

"Willie-boy sent me!" said Bill.

The bartender immediately punched him in the face.

When Bill managed to scrabble his way back up onto the barstool, he had his own fist cocked back to deliver a punch himself.

He found himself looking at the biggest shot glass he'd ever seen, filled with amber fluid that could only be whiskey, alongside a healthy-sized draft beer.

"What?" Bill muttered, head ringing with confusion.

"Code for a practical joke, friend," said the bartender. "All newcomers on Pilgrimworld get it. This is a frontier world, fella. We get kinda rough, but we're good-hearted people too. Enjoy your free drinks."

Bill did not need a second invitation. The whiskey was rotten but alcoholic, the beer flat but cold. But what the hell, this was the frontier. As he sipped and looked into the mirror behind the bar, he saw that Elliot Methadrine was coming through the door. Elliot smiled and pulled up a stool next to the shocked figure of Bill.

"Barman, I'll have whatever my friend here is drinking. And tell him to close his mouth before he catches some flies."

"Ergle!" Bill ergled and clacked his jaw shut. "But you're dead, shot to death in the subway."

"Gee, Bill, you carry the dumb act a long way. Have you forgotten Sir Dudley the Time Portal? He whisked me back to the factory that made the old body, and they ground out another one. He's waiting outside and said to drink up because we have to get going."

"Where to?"

"I'm glad you asked." He took a pair of dark glasses from his pocket and put them on. "You like the shades? They are required where we are going next," said Bgr-Elliot.

"Don't tell me," said Bill. "We're going to a really bright planet."

"No," said Elliot-Chinger. "Actually, Earth has a very *low* IQ. That's where we must go. Earth. Hollywood, California, Bill. Twentieth century! To see a film producer named Slimeball Sid. Who has his own movie production company."

They downed their drinks, waved to the barkeep—who snarled back—and exited.

"Jolly good to see you chappies again," Sir Dudley said. "I think I've worked out the coordinates correctly this time. Shall we leave?"

For once Sir D. got it right. Their feet thudded down on a carpeted floor—and before them was a glass door with the inscription ESS-ESS PRO-DUCTIONS on it. Elliot hauled it open and marched in.

"You got an appointment?" the receptionist yawned, filing a sharp point onto a stiletto fingernail.

"I don't need one. I am Elliot Methadrine."

"Phone first, come back later, get lost."

"The same Elliot Methadrine who sent your employer a check for five hundred thousand bucks."

Her chair crashed to the floor as she hurled herself forward and kissed both of his hands. "In! He's waiting! What a wonderful film it will be! If you will be so kind as to be seated, I will remove Mr. Sid's present appointment and usher you in."

The receptionist hurried down the hall, rotating

her rump quite attractively as she walked on her stiletto heels. Bill watched until she was out of sight, then dropped into a chair. All this rushing about was getting pretty tiring.

"What's this movie stuff about and what happened to the Time Nazis?" asked Bill. "And what about our mission?"

"After we lost you, it hit me," said Elliot-Bgr. "We got all the time there is! I mean, I've got a Portable Time Portal at my disposal! We could deal with the Time Nazis from the future at our own pace. I went back and put the kibosh on the Bloomsbury writers, turned them off the horny-porny books that they were grinding out."

"How'd you do that?" asked Bill.

"That would be singularly difficult to explain to you since I doubt if you have ever even heard of Bloomsbury. The hardest part was reading the copy they produced before the time change started them writing horny-porny. What I did was prey on their weakness for obfuscation and self-indulgence. Slipped them some material on deconstructionism and they were up and running."

"Wasn't there a god involved, helping them along?"

"You smoking something I don't know about? Wait, I did hear something about that on the Deified Network. Creaky old deity named Zoroaster nosing about. We sent him packing. Don't worry any about him."

"Well I'm glad the Nazis are gone—so what's all this about a movie?" said Bill, stretching languorously on the couch.

"Simple." The alien lizard in the Elliot disguise paced on the puce rug. "Bill, you know how long

I've been trying to stop human beings from warring with us Chingers, right?"

"I suppose you have. But you can't blame us. You are heathen alien monsters!"

"Bill, I'm surprised at you!" sniffed Elliot-Bgr, a tear in the corner of his eye. "After all we've been through! After everything I have tried to tell you about peace and no more war. For shame."

"Okay, I forgot. I guess that was just the Trooper brainwashing talking. I should think better of you since you very recently saved my life in the subway."

Elliot nodded. "That's more like it. I *do* think highly of you, Bill. In fact, it occurred to me that you're just perfect for my plan!"

"Your plan? Oh, this movie-star thing. Right."

"Imagine, Bill! With the right technology and a Time Portal like Sir Dudley, I can film the Truth! I'm going to call it THE HUMAN-CHINGER WAR—starring you, Bill. Why, I might even name it after you. BILL, THE GALACTIC HERO. It's going to show you humans for the crazed, warmongering killers that you are—and it's going to make *millions* here on Earth. Not only will it make millions but it will cost next to nothing to make. All the special effects, the blood and drama and death will be *real*. I have a super CD disc here with miles of real footage of real space battles. Kind of a quasi-documentary, Bill! And you're going to be a star. You won't have to be a Starship Trooper anymore! You'll make enough money to buy a whole planet!"

"Barworld?" breathed Bill hopefully.

"If that's what you want," said Elliot Bgr, "that's what you get. Sounds pretty good, huh?"

"Sounds incredibly fabulous," a rotund man with a big cigar in his yob shouted as he came through the door. "Come in and be famous as well as rich. I'm Sid."

CHAPTER 18

THE STRETCHED LIMO SLID THROUGH THE main entrance of SIDSLI PRODUCTIONS and eased to a stop in front of Stage 3.

"This is it," Sid said, waving his cigar in the direction of the sound stage. "We just wrapped yesterday on an incredibly intellectual—but still emotional, you know, for the ladies—blockbuster of a film shyly titled GREEN SLIME CREATURE FROM THE MARTIAN PIT. The sets are there, your leading man is here, the check is in the bank— so let the cameras roll."

He ushered them through the double-doored entrance and into a darkened giant chamber. There were loud clacks as some floods were turned on, and Sid pointed proudly.

"What a beauty! That set cost a bundle, but Sid does nothing on the cheap!"

"Particularly with my money!" Elliot-Bgr observed adroitly.

"You said it—not me! But for quality you gotta pay. And *that* is quality."

"Looks pretty crappy to me," Bill muttered.

"Not only is your lead handsome and articulate—but what a sense of humor!" Sid glowered menacingly at Bill and chomped his cigar—then smiled insincerely, looking very much like a shark. Which, of course, he was in this industry of poor fishes.

The set was a compendium of every dim idea ever conceived by every half-wit that decided to make a bad science fiction film. Of which there were legions. Spark gaps, Vandegraaf generators, impossible machinery, large handles like railroad switching levers on electricity panels. And even more best left undescribed.

"The screen test first," Sid said. "Let's get Bil up there—"

"That's Bill, pronounced with two Ls."

"I'm *sorry*! A sensitive actor, I like that. Communicating passion one moment, compassion the next. My heart goes out to you, Billll! Your career is beginning—and soon your star will shine in the firmament of films outdoing all the other nebulas and stars and asteroids there."

"Your astronomy isn't too good either," Bill said sternly. "But I will teach you a thing or two about the stars, ha-ha, and life and war as well!"

Carried away, he stalked the stage, sucking in his gut, sticking out his chest, seeing not those before him but his soon-to-be career as an actor. Not just an actor but a STAR!

"Camera! Sound! Hit a few more kliegs so I can see the glint in his eye!" shouted Sid. "That's it.

Ready on the right—ready on the left—fire at will!"

It was really pretty boring and dreary and only Bill and Bgr enjoyed it, one dreaming of acting glory, the other of the salvation of his race. Sir Dudley ground his time teeth in agony and instantly fell asleep. Sid had trouble seeing anything through the haze of dollar signs that danced in his eyes. The grips, electricians, carpenters and all the rest paid attention for a while because this was an example of the worst acting they had ever seen. Which was saying a lot. But soon even they were asleep, being silently cursed by the cameraman who was, perforce, forced to remain slightly awake.

No cliche of bad acting went uncliched. No dusty SF prop went unused, no spark of creativity was not instantly snuffed out.

"Take that—and that—you filthy crawling alien life form!" Bill foamed through spittle-licked lips.

"Sid—I gotta see you!"

"Cut!" Sid shouted and foamed himself. "Who is it? What is it? The red light was lit, we're shooting a masterpiece and you walk in!" He shielded his eyes against the light and made out two forms approaching.

"I know you! You are Bluto my driver-bodyguard. You know better than to do this. And if you don't, then *you* know, Sheldon Fastbuck my lifetime friend and accountant."

"It's because I do know," Sheldon said, his words dripping gloom. "Because I know the price of film, cameras, union cameramen—"

"Watch any badmouth crap about the union!" the cameraman shouted.

"I apologize. I'm upset," Sheldon moaned. "I love the unions—my son's an organizer for the longshoremen—but I had to instantly if not sooner bring this heartbreaking news to Sid."

"My darling mother in Miami!—" Sid shrieked in pain.

"—is in perfect health! Like your dear sister and your father in jail. I do not come about health but about something more important. I come about—the bank."

A hush fell. The air chilled. Sid gasped and stepped back. "What about—the bank!" he breathed hoarsely.

"The bank called—"

"Tell me!"

"They called about a check!"

"Don't spare me—a little check?"

"A *big* check. The check this momser gave you. It was—a *rubber* check!"

"Bounced!" Sid screamed.

"As high as the moon."

Now Sid's voice was cold as death. He turned, pointed a cruel finger. "Bluto—*kill!* These vermin—out!"

Big as he was, and heavy as he was, Bluto was greased lightning. Even as the word *out* was echoing from the rafters, he had Elliot-Bgr by the seat of the trousers and was hurling him through the emergency exit door.

"I say!" Sir Dudley said, waking with a start. "Hold on—you can't do that."

"Bluto already done it buddy—so don't interfere," Bluto grimaced, seizing up Bill even as he spoke. Bill struggled against the steel grip to no avail. Sir D stepped forward to complain just as Bluto pulled Bill back in a swinging arc—then hurled him at the door.

But Sir Dudley was in the way. He recoiled, but it was too late.

Bill was thrown through the Time Portal and into the uncharted wastes of convoluted time.

CHAPTER **19**

WHEN BILL AWOKE, HE IMMEDIATELY noted two things.

The first was that he didn't have a headache.

The second was that he was stone cold sober.

Both of these facts were quite remarkable. He felt quite good physically, rested and fit. He felt in top shape, like he used to feel back on a holiday on Phigerinadon II after a good sleep-in. In fact, he would have just lain where he was, reveling in his good feelings, were it not for the fact that he suddenly and unequivocally realized that he hadn't the faintest idea where the hell he was!

Bill opened his eyes.

Above him was a metal wall of riveted panels. A soft alarm rang behind him, and he angled his gaze to take in some kind of instrument panel with dials and digital readouts.

He heard the sound of soft footsteps padding toward him.

"Well, then! You're awake," said a clear, precise voice. "How are we feeling today?"

"Okay," said Bill suspiciously, noncommittally. He looked up at the speaker, saw a nondescript man in a short haircut, a bland angular face wearing a doctor's smock. The man carried a clipboard, and this he consulted.

"Well, guy, whoever you are, you were quite a mess, internally. Trooper's tummy we call it. We can't have that kind of thing, no sir. So we cleaned you up chemically. You're no longer physically addicted to alcohol. That liver of yours isn't in great shape, but we didn't have another on hand, so you're going to have to make do with it. Just no more booze for you. Which is okay, since it's unlikely you'll get any where they're sending you."

"*Where* are they sending me?" Bill demanded, sitting up in bed. All about him was the telltale antiseptic smell of a sick bay.

"From the hospital the Troopers are usually sent to Deathworld 69. And you're a Trooper all right. We know that. Who else would have vat-grown surgically implanted tusks, two right arms and a metal foot? You belong to us, body and soul. But the question is, just who *are* you."

"Trooper Bill! That's who I am. I'm on assignment with the Galactic Bureau of Investigation. What year is this?" Bill was unused to thinking and speaking clearly, but it certainly helped in this odd situation.

"9435.24 Standard Galactic," said the man.

"That's about two years ago!"

The doctor gave him a puzzled look. "Two years

ago. I don't understand what you mean."

"Two years from when I go back in time. Like I say, I'm undercover for the GBI."

"I repeat, Trooper. Who *are* you?"

"Bill. Trooper Bill."

"Yes. So your retinal patterns and fingerprints would have us believe. However, we checked the records. Trooper Bill is presently recovering from foot surgery. In fact, anticipating your awakening, we've got him on Visual Ultra-Light High-Speed Space-Transmission Television." The doctor snapped his fingers. Two orderlies pushed over a television set. The doctor turned it on.

The picture was of a bar. Sitting at the bar, in front of a drink, Bill immediately recognized a man who was clearly himself.

"Pardon me," said the doctor to the television screen. "Pardon me, Trooper!"

The man at the bar blinked, yawned, then looked up blearily toward the TV camera, toward them. "Wuzzsha?" He inquired incoherently.

"What is your name, Trooper?"

"Bill. Trooper Bill. Thash's with two L's, and don't you forget it, bowbhead . . ."

"Doctor Bowbhead! I mean Doctor Magnus Fraud! Intergalactic Medical Corps. Sit to attention, shut up—and listen. We've got a slight problem, Trooper Bill. There's a trooper here that claims *he's* Trooper Bill. We thought you might help us out."

"What?" said the man at the bar, working to understand what was happening. "I'm *here!*"

"Do you recognize this man beside me?"

The man at the bar shook his head to focus his eyes, blinked a few times, then reached for his beer.

"Never saw'm before. Too ugly to be me." He drained the glass.

Bill was aghast. "Hey, listen, you sodden moron. It's me! Don't you recognize me?"

"No chance," said the younger edition of Bill. "You *look* a little like me. But I'm here, you're there. Goodbye."

"Have you ever been cloned, Trooper Bill?" the Doctor asked the television screen.

"Not that I know of."

"I see. We found this man unconscious because he seemed to have landed on his head—and we don't know where he came from. Are you *sure* you can't help us?"

"Nope. If you decide to dismantle him, though, I want one of his feet."

"I got foot trouble just like you, idiot!" said Bill Prime. "Here, look! This got shot off on Veneria. Remember?"

"Hey. Veneria! That's something. I got mine shot off on Veneria too."

"Of course you did—because you're me! Only two years ago. I mean, I'm you—two years from now. I'm traveling in time!"

"Yeah? Pull the other one."

There was a sudden transmission problem. Bill lifted a finger as though about to say something—

And then he keeled over backward on his barstool, falling into an unconscious heap on the floor.

"Okay. That's enough, more than enough," said the doctor. "He didn't recognize you. You *must* be an impostor. You're human enough, though."

He went to switch off the television.

"No, wait! Bill!" cried Bill. "Wake up, Bill. You're my only *hope*. I don't want to go to Deathworld 69,

Bill!" His only answer was a snore.

"That's it," the doctor said as he snapped off the set. "Time's awasting. You are off to Deathworld 69." The doctor nodded at the orderlies, who immediately applied the necessary restraints to the errant and unidentified Trooper.

"Take this cannon fodder and chain him up, lads. He'll do his duty to the Emperor, all right—and probably die horribly doing it!"

Bill struggled, but to no avail. Soon the orderlies were dragging him off.

"Oh, and Trooper Not-Bill," said the doctor, wagging a finger. "Just remember. No more drinking. It's bad for your health."

The MPs grabbed him with great glee and, kicking and screaming, hauled him onto the deathship that was his destination, chaining him firmly into place in a dank and awful level. Only then did Bill finally remember about the bracelet that Bgr and Sir Dudley had given him.

Groaning, he turned over on the bed of straw where he'd been hurled and examined his wrist. Sure enough, there was the bracelet, all right. But where were his Time/Space pals, who'd promised to come and get him if he went astray?

Then he remembered.

Bgr had said that this thing wouldn't work around impervium—and this whole time he'd been in nothing but impervium spaceships and transport boats.

They couldn't get him *out* because there was no way they knew he was *here!*

Bill lay back in the straw with a sigh of despair. After all this work, here he was, stuck in a boat, headed toward a Deathworld, probably much like Veneria, where he'd blown his foot to smithereens to get off. Only the type of Chinger-battling he was going to do on Some Godforsaken Planet—Deathworld 69—would have no such escape. If he blew off his feet, the Troopers would just make him fight on his knees.

Bill lay moaning in the dank, smelly straw.

Oh, what a life!

And he was going to have to deal with the whole trip *stone cold sober!*

The days crawled slowly and arthritically by.

Bill subsisted on his old and all-too-familiar diet of absolutely chemically pure water in which were dissolved eighteen amino acids, sixteen vitamins, eleven mineral salts, a fatty acid ester and glucose.

It was hideously repulsive—but it kept him alive.

Without any comix to read or anything alcoholic to drink, he soon grew bored beyond words. The only thing he could do was to relive his life in flashbacks, and since his memory was so poor because of all the years of drinking, this took about forty-four minutes.

On the hundred-and-second reliving of his life, Bill became so unutterably bored that he finally gave in to the Unthinkable.

He pulled his ear and accessed his lobe implant so he could have someone to talk to. Even if the someone was a pretty artificial artificial intelligence. He was immediately rewarded with a wail of country and western music.

"Hi there, pardner! This here AI was worrying some since you-all warn't accessing me like you used to."

Bill didn't bother telling the thing that he really had forgotten about the implant, which was a marvel of bio-electronics directly plugged into Bill's cerebellum. He had forgotten that it also had a store of ethnic music it insisted on playing. But it also had an amazing database of knowledge and some intelligence, and could also be used as a handy pocket calculator. He had forgotten too how irritating the thing was. It was apparently equipped with all manner of sensor devices hooked to Bill's nervous system: nanochip memory, a rudimentary artificial intelligence, a nasal voice simulator. He cursed the demented programmer who had designed the system, who also had a love for the ethnic music of long-vanished Earth. He must have tapped a digitized databank from one of the ancient spacers and had dumped it into the RAM in Bill's ear. But he had written such crappy software that bits of the music leaked through into the rest of the programs.

"Give me the word, pard," the AI whined nasally. "Where we at? What's going on? How's the mission going? You got that Time Hole problem straightened out? Hope so. I'd like to go back to central."

Bill almost turned the thing back off, but then he remembered how bored and miserable he was. Maybe he could learn to like the rotten ethnic music that was playing forever in the background.

Maybe he could learn to enjoy getting repeatedly kicked in the head by robo-mules, too. Well, at least it would make him enjoy the silence a lot more, when he finally had to switch the implant off.

"I'm chained on a starship going to Deathworld 69—Some Godforsaken Planet," Bill explained self-pityingly. "And I've been kicked back in time as well. It's going to be two years until I have the

interview with J. Edgar Insufledor. Two years until
they put you into me. Two years and many light-
years away."

No immediate response. The news had clearly put
the implant into a state of electronic shock.

"That's a bummer, old hoss," it said finally. "Talk
about being at the wrong place at the wrong time!"

"I'll say."

"Trooper Bill. I detect something quite different
about you."

"What? Complete and total misery as opposed to
mere black depression?"

"No. You seem, I don't quite know how to spit
this out—but y'all seem sober."

"That's because I haven't been drinking lately, you
idiot AI. Drinking nothing except the sludge they call
food here."

"Good buddy, it's more than that. You seem . . .
well, now that I check my neurofilament registers, I
see that they show the same horse sense too—your
IQ has improved!"

"My what?"

"Your intelligence quotient, sonny! Not that ah
wants to lecture, but—" There was a quick burst of
a tarantella and the AI's accent changed again. "I'ma
talkin' bought how you cabeesh mathematics, science, philosophy, linguistics! Do a queeck check—
Mamma Mia!—you gotta da IQ she go from about
a 90 to well over 170!"

Captivated by this discovery the AI gave a quick
squirt of Country Gardens that segued into Green-
sleeves. "It does appear that the drinking you were
so skilled at must have been suppressing your intelligence. According to my records, you were a farmer,
a robo-mule jockey, with a burning desire to become

a Fertilizer Technician. Maybe it was the chemicals in that fertilizer that suppressed the growth of your neo-cortex. In any event, it now seems to be growing at an increasing rate. Perhaps you received a significant temporal radiation blast during these recent travels in time as well."

Bill related the whole sad story from the elevated heights of Barworld to the present depths of the dismal starship.

"I must say, that's rather grim stuff."

"Now—any ideas for the future?" asked Bill.

"You've tried breaking your chain and escaping?"

"I see why they call your intelligence artificial. Think, you electronic nitwit—if I broke the chain, where would I go to? We're in the middle of deep space, on our way to Some Godforsaken Planet."

"Deathworld 69. I know. Depressing. Look at it this way, though. At least you'll have a chance there."

"A very small one. I've been to Veneria. That's a Deathworld. Troopers last a week there, tops. Why do you think they've got people chained up in here? They'd try to mutiny for sure. *They* know where they're headed."

A few moans sounded in the distance, as though doomed Troopers had been listening and were reminded of their fates.

"Dreadful. But presumably the voyage takes a while."

"Presumably." Bill felt the stubble on his cheeks and then the growth on his head. "I've already been here a while."

"We must do our best to keep you sane when all about you are losing their heads."

"You can start by not playing that crummy music all the time then!"

"Be delighted to. And as long as there's nothing else for you to do, we might as well educate you."

"Educate me?"

"Yes. You should realize that stored in my data banks are all of the encyclopedias of the galaxy, the technical texts—everything needed for a complete education. And, dare I say it, I'm rather a pretty good teacher, too."

"All in all, I think I'd rather have a beer."

"All in all, I'd rather be listening to the only two kinds of music in the galaxy—country and western. Cheers."

A little *pop*, and the voice was gone.

Silence.

"Well, bowb you too, buddy," huffed Bill, folding his arms stubbornly over his chest. But then, after just a few moments of dead silence and boredom, he yanked once again on his earlobe.

"Are you there, old buddy? Sorry I got carried away. Yeah, sure. Let's talk. You teach, I'll learn. What do you say?"

Nothing.

Bill yanked harder on his earlobe. This time he got an ear-splitting jolt of jazz.

"Okay. Groovy, dude. You wanna start with 'A'— or do you just wanna go potluck?"

"Potluck sounds good," Bill said, his salivary glands watering at the gustatory allusion.

And so, with the AI's help, Bill learned, sifting through the memory banks containing the knowledge and wisdom of the ages.

Bill learned the history of the human race. He learned the stories of the great religions. He learned about the development of science. Soon he was engaging in long Socratic dialogues with the AI, and when he was through with his course in philosophy, he engaged in a debate with the earlobe implant over the respective merits of Kant's ethics as opposed to Kierkegaard's epistemology.

Bill learned biology, mathematics and advanced mathematics. He learned physics from the Newtonian principles well through quantum mechanics. He even began to understand how starship drives worked, which was a considerable accomplishment since even the creators of those drives hadn't the foggiest. Bill learned xenobiology, and he learned xenosociology and xenosewage principles. Bill finally began to understand some of the beauties of the universe. He understood Bgr's society now, and saw the tragedy that had visited the Chinger worlds in the guise of humanity.

For weeks upon weeks, Bill learned, sucking up knowledge as a sponge sucks up water.

When the starship landed, the AI, who had been sorting through plans of survival, came up with one so simple it worked. There were mounds of kicked-up straw and Bill burrowed beneath the filthy stuff. Sure enough, when the imprisoned cannon-fodder Troopers were herded out, the guards simply passed by Bill without seeing him in the darkness.

This was the beginning of a new existence for Bill. His sordid environment didn't matter. Bill discovered that he loved knowledge. And adored wisdom. All the subjects that the AI implant taught him. Suddenly, the universe was a great and wonderful place, full of fascinating truths and incredible mysteries.

Bill began to marvel at the secrets of life itself, and

with the help of the implant began to piece together all of the parts of that great alchemical riddle that had stumped all of mankind, perhaps even all of *being* kind throughout the ages:

The Meaning of Life itself!

His mind and intellect marvelously expanded, Bill came upon a simple truth that had somehow eluded the philologists, philosophers, and great theological thinkers throughout history.

Life had a meaning, all right.

But because it was hard to figure out, you just couldn't put it into normal GalSpeak words.

No, the Meaning of Life, to be properly understood, needed its own language mathematical. Since necessity is the mother of invention—no one knows who the father is—he invented that language. It was directed toward a single goal: to ferret out and elucidate those elusive little morsels of meaning that comprised the greater whole. The Meaning of Life.

Finally, after weeks, months, yes even *years*, two to be precise, Bill was able to boil down all the wisdom and knowledge into one short mathematical statement. He scratched it on the wall with a nail, read and admired it. This was it. The meaning of life. At last. When the time came, he would share this knowledge with the galaxy.

Roughly translated in GelSpeak this translation read:

Life = Bowb.

Life doesn't mean bowb. Brief. Profound.

Brilliant.

Bill had no idea where he was when he wrote down the equation. They had landed many times during his imprisonment, and Bill had always hidden under the filthy straw, always to be passed over. He'd lost count of the days that had passed, because there were no days—only an eternal dimness, punctuated by the moans and chain-clankings of the imprisoned Troopers.

He admired the equation from all sides. His mind became aglow—no, absolutely incandescent! He was afire with this sudden Truth, and that fire raged through him with a fierce burning clarity that would solve all the problems in the universe.

The Meaning of Life was the solution to all of the galaxy's ills! It would put a stop to all pain, all suffering. If he could only get off this hellboat, and communicate it to the governments of the Chingers and to the Emperor himself, then the Chinger and the Human Empires would at long last be at peace.

No more Galactic Troopers!

No more war!

No more hate and fear and blood and death and mayhem! No more reason to drink yourself to oblivion. It would be a universe of peace, of music and art and literature! A universe of cooperation, of universal good.

"Life is incredible!" he confided to the AI. "Only I suspect that I would enjoy it even more if I could get something decent to eat and get off this ship!"

"You're right. But how?"

Bill didn't know. He therefore turned his burgeoning, light-filled mind toward other pursuits. Since the normal galactic would take a lifetime just mastering the principles of his equation, let alone comprehending its subtleties, Bill began to work on the problem of how exactly to translate the Meaning of Life into words that normal people could understand. This was no easy proposition, and he came to a number of dead ends before he even saw a hope of accomplishing his goals. For he well realized that if he could not communicate the Meaning of Life to others, then it could not exercise its healing powers.

And then one day, while he was working on a particularly difficult exegesis, a man ran past him, tripping over the chain that attached him to the wall, breaking the chain in two.

Bill had a sudden attack of semi-*deja vu*.

CHAPTER 20

BILL STOOD UP.

"Out of the way, motherbowber!" said the man who had inadvertently freed him. "I gotta get off this tub!"

Bill tried to speak, but he'd done so little of it in the last two years that he delivered this: "Slowly I turn," he rumbled deeply. "Step by step . . . inch by inch. . . . "

"You got a problem, bozo? I sure do! I'm outta here!"

Bill lifted his leg, from which the old broken chain depended. Sure, enough, it was true! "I'm free!" he said. "I don't believe it! You've *freed* me! I've been in this starship, forgotten, for years. And you've freed me. How ever can I thank you?"

"You can just move it! I've gotta get down this ladder!"

A loudspeaker rattled. "Two minutes till closing of hatch. Next stop: Some Godforsaken Planet!"

"Oh no! That's Deathworld 69! There is death, only death there!" Bill fell to his knees, blubbering miserably before the man.

"Get outta my way!"

"Please, sir! I'll give you the Secret to the Universe! I know the meaning of Life itself!"

"Look, butt-head, I don't care if you've got the keys to the captain's liquor cabinet. This boat's gonna blow soon, and I'm not going to be on it!"

"I'm not lying!"

"You can get out of the way, buddy. I got to get down this ladder."

A loudspeaker rattled. "One minute till closing of hatch. Next stop: Some Godforsaken Planet!"

Terror shot through the strange Trooper.

"I'm not lying!"

"Thirty seconds to hatch closing," the speaker voice said. "Last chance for flight insurance. A mere ten million credits per head. Twenty-nine seconds . . . ."

This, thought Bill, was getting awfully familiar.

And so was this guy here!

"I said, bowb-for-brains, get out of my way!"

Bill received a quick, hard shove. He fell back and back—and then the floor seemed to open up beneath him. He scrabbled for purchase, seized the rungs of a ladder—and the thing buckled and fell down with him.

He hit the floor hard, but he knew exactly what he had to do. Without hesitation, despite the pain coursing through his body, he pulled himself up and headed for what, instinctively, he knew was the way out.

Sure enough, soon he saw the outline of the door to freedom. It was a hatch, and daylight shone through, smelly and smoggy but daylight nonetheless. Almost blinded by the light, Bill staggered down the gangplank.

Free, he thought. *Free!*

But free—where?

"Hey, Trooper. Where the hell do you think you're going?" demanded a guard.

"Where am I?" asked Bill.

"You're really out of it, aren't you! You're at the Happy Trails Spaceport on Jinx Ether Force Base. You're *trying* to get off this Starship BEELZEBUB. So who the hell are you?"

It all came back to him, all of it. With his new intelligence, he was able to see exactly what had happened.

He'd gone back in time, gone back the hard way—

And bumped into himself.

He knew immediately what he had to say.

"I'm Lieutenant Brandox. That's who I am!"

"Great. That means that the Trooper found who he's looking for, huh? Where the hell is he?"

"He's on his way. He should be out any moment now."

The guard examined his watch. "He'd better shake it! This thing's about ready to go."

"Don't worry," said Bill. "He'll make it. Just . . . ."

Sure enough, at exactly three seconds before it was too late, he saw himself barreling and rolling down the gangplank. The Trooper that was his past self rolled to a halt at the bottom of the ramp.

"Hey, guy," said the guard. "This guy Brandox?"

Bill stared down at his past self, with all the beseeching he could muster from his reddened eyeballs.

He met his own gaze, and something strange clicked.

"Yeah. That's him. He's coming with me."

"Well, I suggest you get in your gravcar and get the hell outta here because these things go off in an explosion that cinders living things for yards around." The guard immediately started running away, leaving them alone.

Bill looked around. Sure enough, there was the gravcar he remembered. He jumped into the back seat.

Grumpily, the before-Bill leaped into the driver's seat and gunned the anti-grav repulsors. "I don't know why I'm doing this. I just don't know," he said as they raced away.

"You won't be sorry, Bill," said Bill. "I promise you."

Bill heard the BEELZEBUB behind them, starting to blast off. Then he felt something tugging at his wrist.

The bracelet . . . it was activating. Behind the impervium shielding of the BEELZEBUB it wouldn't work. But out here, it had shot off a signal through time and space—

A signal to Sir Dudley and Elliot-Bgr.

Sure enough, before he even had a moment to extrapolate mentally from this thought, the two of them materialized. They hung suspended in the air, Elliot waving him toward the time gate.

Bill didn't even wait for an invitation. Long hair flapping, he hurled himself from the speeding gravcar directly into Sir Dudley the Time Portal. Elliot-Bgr and a much-changed Bill disappeared, leaping back into the future.

* * *

And to Hellworld.

"Where are we?" Bill gasped, coughing as he inhaled the smoky, polluted air. Lightning shot from dark clouds, fetid warm rain fell on the decayed, crumbling city that surrounded them. Murky figures shuffled through the gloom as distant thunder rumbled.

"You might very well ask," Sir Dudley sniffed. "While you were doing whatever you were doing—and judging by the way you look it was surely an interesting experience—Elliot and I decided enough was enough. Even restoring the Bloomsbury group to their boring epistles did not remove the Nazi menace completely. So Hellworld must still exist. Using the most sophisticated tracking and computational techniques, I located this un-descended testicle of time. A recursive loop that was originating all the trouble in time. We are here now to eliminate it forever."

"Sounds reasonable," Bill observed. "Investigate, elucidate, cogitate, eliminate."

"Gee, Bill, all of a sudden you are talking funny," Elliot-Bgr said. "What *did* happen to you while you were away?"

"I will be happy to elucidate after we terminate the present operation."

"Yeah—gee—wow," Elliot-Bgr muttered, shaking his head in mystification as he turned to Sir Dudley. "What facts do you have on this place?"

"Very little. Planet of doom and despair. I get Nazi readings and a strong smell of hippies. Also, I must add, a sonic boom of horny-porny. Yes, there it is—we are there at last—the home of horny-porny and horny-porny fandom! And I must say, Bill, indeed I must, that you certainly look the part!"

Bill caught a glimpse of himself in the cracked window of a decaying building. He could not help but gasp. He looked a great deal like the guy who had tried to murder him on board the starship to Barworld!

Shaggy, uncombed hair hung down from the top of his head. He had a long beard and mustache. His clothes were ragged and tattered.

"Disgusting—but an excellent disguise for this operation, is it not?" he commented.

Elliot-Bgr turned up his nose in disgust. "Yeah, fine, Bill. You better get yourself a bath though, huh Trooper? I always said from the beginning that all bowby humans have B.O. Chingers can't sweat. Chingers forever!—but you're particularly offensive today, Bill!"

"I'll agree completely," said Sir Dudley.

"I do apologize, gentlemen. Dreadfully sorry, but I *have* been lying in a prison ship for two years, so I would appreciate a bit more understanding."

Elliot-Bgr shook his head sorrowfully. Or was the shaking of the head a Chinger expression of sarcastic mirth? "That must have been rough, Bill. Glad you got out, though. Gee—we were combing the timeways for you, guy. Just what did you do to while away the time?"

"Well, I'm sober," said Bill. "I'm sober and I don't want a drink. And with the help of that implant J. Edgar Insufledor gave me, I am now educated!"

"No!" said Sir Dudley.

"Yes, and I have come up with the Meaning of Life!"

"You're pulling my tail!" said the Chinger.

"Of course, to do so I had to develop my own mathematical language. And to understand the Meaning of Life, you have to understand the equations," Bill said.

"Gee—why don't we get you a bath before our first lesson?"

"Yes, and then let's deal with these hippies and Time Nazis!"

"It's really worth it. It will solve all the problems of the universe—you'll join me in this great understanding."

The trio hurried along to find a hotel room. The Time Nazis and the hippies from Hellworld could wait a while longer; Bill needed a bath!

As they strode along, Bill noticed that all of the natives, women and men alike, looked much like him. Shaggy hair, ratty clothes. However, they all had something that Bill did not: a propeller beanie perched atop their heads.

"Ah ha!" he said. "Yes! The emblem of the hardcore aficionado of horny-porny! So this must be the planet that they migrated to in hopes of fleeing persecution!"

"Gee, Bill, we just said all that!"

"Ah!" said Bill, taking in the sights. "Ah ha!" After such a long time in a dank, dark hole it was incredibly invigorating and intriguing to have this wide array of sensory input. And what *fascinating* stuff as well! "This entire city seems built like a gigantic convention center! And the indigenous population seems to be involved in one long never-ending horny-porny convention, an overripe tradition established somewhere in the lost mists of time."

"Let's get that hotel room and that bath!" said Elliot-Bgr. "You can make the intelligent observations later!"

They wended their way past huckster rooms jammed with books, cheap jewelry, horny-porny magazines and the oddest effluvia that Bill had ever

seen. Long-haired Hellworld hippies marched around
in barbarian outfits, half-naked slave girl disguises,
sadomasochistic bordello madams with whips and
other interesting outfits. They walked past rooms
filled with hippies listening to horny-porny person-
ages prattle on about buggering, battering, wanking,
pranking and other colorful concepts the mind cannot
stomach. They walked past great halls filled with art
shows, filled with pictures that looked as though ripped
straight from Bill's Three-Dee collection of
horny-porny comix.

The pre-educated Bill might have been quite impressed, but the present, superacademic Bill,
equipped with the equivalent of ten PhDs from Ox-
ford, three from Harvard and a honorary kiss on the
forehead from the president of Berkeley, was ap-
palled.

"My goodness. What perverted taste! I can only
imagine the horrors perpetrated by their fiction!"

For Bill, in his relaxing hours from all his learning,
had also read all the great classics—from BEOWULF
through Shakespeare to ABDUCTION: THE UFO
CONSPIRACY. So he well knew the difference between Quality and Sleazy Popular Trash. Bill's fond-
est hope now, after imparting the Meaning of Life to
the inept incompetents of the universe, was to write
his memoirs—if only to attempt to remember what
had actually happened to him. Clearly, it was the
Sleazy Popular Trash these horny-porny hippies on
Hellworld consumed.

"Come on Bill," said Elliot-Bgr. "This stuff may
stink all right. But right now, you stink worse!"

The trio obtained a room with a bath and there
immersed Bill in a bathtub. It took five separate bath-
tubs full of hot water to scrub the grime from Bill's

body. It was decided, however, to keep his hair and beard, since that way the group could be much better disguised as they sought out the source of the horny-porny infection.

To aid their disguise, Sir Dudley no longer looked like a Time Portal but was disguised as a torture master complete with whips and molten lead pot. Elliot-Bgr was most fetching as a half-naked Babylonian harlot.

"Shall we proceed, gentlemen?" Bill asked. For, indeed, he was very proud of his newly acquired intelligence. He had, finally, a purpose to his existence.

He was not only going to save the universe, he was going to give to it the meaning that had enriched his own soul so much!

CHAPTER **21**

"YEAH! WHAT CAN I DO FOR *YOUSE* GUYS?" the security guard wanted to know. He was a big, muscular moron wearing a polka-dot propeller beanie and a blue uniform with epaulets, a gun holster and, of course, a gun. Also, his fly was open.

"Good afternoon," said Bill with a polite bow. "We are horny-porny fans who have been directed here to meet with Publishers on High of super horny-porny. Which floor?"

"Guess you'd be looking for Galactic Horn-Porn Publications on the ninth and tenth floors. That's where the Doc hangs out. He's in charge of the operation. Writers and editors on the seventh and eighth. Regular elevators are on the fritz today. You're going to have to use the service elevator!"

"Thank you, kind sir!" said Bill, thrilled not only with his expanded vocabulary, but with his new set of manners. "You are a gentleman and a scholar."

"Just down the hall there," the guard said, pointing. "Right by those boxes of freeze-dried horny-porny writer brains."

Bill and company trooped on down to the indicated elevator at the end of the hall. Sure enough, stacked haphazardly beside it were boxes marked: "FRAGILE—INSTANT WRITER BRAINS. Just add hot water and stir-fry."

"Interesting," said Bill. "I always *did* wonder where they got their crazy ideas!"

After a long wait, the elevator finally arrived. They hopped in and rode it to the ninth floor. They disembarked. Bill's ears were immediately assaulted by the sound of computer keyboards clacking. Bill looked in a door and his eyes were met with a dreadful sight.

Row upon row of word processors filled the large room, and at these word processors were chained men and women, bent over the keys, working away diligently on rows of phosphor-dot prose. Coffee drips were plugged directly into the veins of their arms: obscene black plasma. Their shirts hung in bloody rags, and welts glistened on their backs. Up and down the rows stalked muscle-bound guards holding whips, ready to flay the soul who was spotted pausing too long between sentences. Upon the sides of the desks were piled what could only be the payment these poor slaves received for their literary efforts: pennies.

"Gee," said Elliot-Bgr. "Talk about word processing, huh?"

"EDITORIAL DEPARTMENT," Bill read on a sign. "This way. I guess that's where Doctor Kraft-Nibbling, Jr.[10] hangs out. Then you are certain that in this disgusting slice of time he is the one behind this business? I see no evidence of National Socialism here. This looks like pure capitalism!"

"I know, I know!" said Sir Dudley. "I am puzzled. But we must confront this man! These atrocities must be stopped. The treatment of writers is most revolting. Even if they are clones, they should not be treated so badly!"

"That's right!" said Elliot-Bgr. "We *worship* and *adore* our writers. They receive vast honor and love, and get preferential treatment in all matters. Particularly communal orgies."

Bill shook his head. "You're right. I do believe I have a new cause—Writers' Rights. Which is opportune, since I intend to become a writer myself!"

"Indeed," said Sir Dudley. "Do you intend to write a Bartender's Guide to Drunks? As experienced—not told to the author."

"I have forsaken alcohol and now drink purely from the Fountain of Truth!" said Bill.

By this time they had reached Kraft-Nibbling's offices. They did not bother to knock, but barged directly in.

"Who are you?" demanded a secretary.

"We're here to see Kraft-Nibbling!" said Elliot-Bgr, taking out his blaster. "Get him or else!"

The secretary hit an intercom key. "Doctor Kraft-Nibbling," she said. "I believe we have a few irate readers in the reception room!"

"Nazis?" said Doctor Kraft-Nibbling.

"Worse," said Bill. "*Time* Nazis."

Doctor Shelley D. Kraft-Nibbling, Jr.[10] was absolutely pale. He had to sit down in an armchair. "Look, guys. Bill, Elliot-Bgr, Sir Dudley the Time Portal. I have to admit that I may be a little ruthless.

I may have sent my horny-porny hippie fans back through time to change the course of fictional history. I may treat my writers like dirt and pay them pennies. But Time Nazis? Never! I only want to promote my business and spread the joys of horny-porny throughout the ages. But Time Nazis! I don't know how this has happened! I can't possibly understand where things went wrong—*if*, in fact, what you tell me is true!"

Bill eyed him suspiciously. "Of course it's true. You don't believe us? You want *proof*?"

In fact, Bill didn't trust the guy at all. Maybe it was the slicked-back hair. Maybe it was the snazzy, svelte look. Maybe it was the snakeskin shoes. Maybe it was the Eau-de-Shark that hung about him like a miasma. Mostly, though, it was because he reminded Bill of a lawyer, with his sharp nose and his glib, feral look.

It was a fact that the Emperor had, of course in a mood of philanthropy, taken Shakespeare's advice and destroyed all the lawyers in the known universe during The Great Shyster Purge. However, this had only been a few years before, so Bill well remembered what the breed had been like. In fact, doubtless it had been a military lawyer who had drafted the induction contract he had been induced to sign back on Phigerinadon II.

Still, he'd always been a fan of horny-porny comix, so the Doc couldn't be *all* bad!

"Look," said Kraft-Nibbling. "I *like* you guys, I really do. I can tell you're my sort of people!"

"How come one of your Time Hippies tried to kill Bill and me then?" said Elliot-Bgr.

"Clearly the guy was a little too fanatical," admitted the man. "But I most certainly did not order him to kill anybody! In fact, I want only peace, prosperity, happiness and steady selling lines—with very few returns to the publishers." He looked around. "What I don't see, gentlemen, is *any* sign of your so-called Time Nazis!"

The office intercom chose that moment to squawk.

"Pardon me, Doctor Kraft-Nibbling," said the secretary's voice. "But Mr. Shickelgruber would like to speak to you."

"That's a familiar-sounding name!" said Sir Dudley.

"Tell him, Edna, that I've got an important meeting to deal with at the moment and—"

The secretary's voice sounded extremely stressed. "I don't believe he's going to take 'no' for an answer...."

The door flung open.

A man wearing boots, a gray uniform, black armbands and a little black mustache stormed into the room, waving a Luger pistol.

"Put your hands in the air or you *vill die!*" said the Nazi.

"That's it!" said Sir Dudley. "Wasn't 'Shickelgruber' that chap Hitler's real name?"

EPILOGUE

"THAT WAS A GOOD SHOT, BGR," BILL said. "A single blaster blast and Hitler was no more. And it's nice to see you out of that Elliot disguise and back in four-armed green the way you should look."

"Once he was gone, the time track became clear," Sir Dudley said. "I traced the trail right back to where they plucked him from the bunker before he snuffed it."

"What I liked even better was how all the hippies and Hellworld and everything vanished when the time line was destroyed," Bgr the Chinger said. "Gee—we gotta be grateful to you, Sir D, for some fast thinking and instant Time Portal operation."

"You're too kind, dear boy. Just doing my duty."

"Above and beyond the call of duty. And abover and beyonder, picking Barworld as our destination!"

"Seemed an obvious spot to celebrate."

Not to Bill. He sat, mournfully looking at a glass of lemonade. "Life doesn't mean bowb," he kept repeating. "Life doesn't mean bowb."

Well, mission complete, he thought to himself. *Here I am, back at Uncle Nancy's Cross-Dressing Bar, in a nice little summer ensemble, and the universe is safe from Time Nazis, and I know the Meaning of Life. Why, then, do I feel like what Life doesn't mean?*

Bill pondered that thought.

"Glad to be back in business, boys!" said Uncle Nancy, supplying them all with a fresh round of drinks. To celebrate, Uncle Nancy was wearing a delightful blue gown with spangles. A feather boa was wrapped around his neck. "Glad to have it back in good shape with booze and no ironpumpers. Hey, Bill. You're not drinking your lemonade. Can I get you a man's drink—on the house? How about a nice foamy mug of Halcyonian home brew? So much alcohol it leaks through the cask!"

Bill's salivary glands gushed, but Bill shook his head. "No thanks, my friend. I am off alcohol for life." He patted his much-improved liver. "Not only must I think about my physical health—but it is my mental health that is in greatest danger. My great intelligence would instantly vanish if ethyl alcohol assaulted my brain cells ever again."

"Whatever. Say, that was a pretty good job you guys did with those Time Nazis. You guys get free drinks all night!"

Bgr was drinking suds with great enthusiasm out of a glass almost as big as he was. "Gee, thanks! Now all we have to do is to go back and stop the Human-Chinger war and everything will be hunky-dory!"

"No way!" said Sir Dudley. "I've given up transporting people back and forth in time. No more changes! Those Time Nazis might come back if we do any more tinkering. Who knows. Maybe Hitler

had more than one brain—and it's lurking somewhere out there in the galaxy!"

The Time Portal shivered.

"Oh well," said Bgr. "Gee—it was worth a try.
Well, nice to drink with you guys, have a temporary
truce anyway."

They continued joking and chewing over their adventures together, while Bill sipped his lemonade,
musing. The thing was, if life didn't mean *bowb*, and
bowb was what you'd known all your life, then
where did you go from there? This equation he had
developed was all well and good, and it was nice to
be super-intelligent. But what *for?*

In fact, the more he thought about it, from the
viewpoint of intelligence, the darker, more fright-
ening and hideous this repellent universe became!

Not only that, this intelligence was making him
positively neurotic. At least when you were stupid
you didn't worry about much. All Bill had worried
about before was first staying alive, then perhaps
where his next beer was coming from.

A truly eloquent, simple life indeed.

Suddenly, Bill was aware of a huge mug of beer
being slid under his nose. The aroma of yummy hops
and malt was almost too much for him. He looked
up and saw Uncle Nancy's smiling face.

"What's this?" said Bill.

"Aw, go on, Bill. One won't hurt you. Have some
fun. You're spoiling the party."

"No," said Bill. "This lemonade will do. What I
need is some stimulating conversation. Let's talk
about literature, Uncle Nancy. Or perhaps philosophy. I think that—"

A commotion at the entrance distracted him. As

one, Bill and his friends at the bar turned around to see a group of Troopers, not wearing dresses, parade into the bar. Leading them was none other than J. Edgar Insufledor, wearing a trench coat.

"Bill!" said the Galactic Bureau of Investigation department head in his bluff, gravelly voice. "Bill! Your report is inadequate! Mission successful? What does *that* mean? And where is Elliot Methadrine!"

"Ha ha, you silly old coot!" said Elliot-Bgr, hopping up and down a little drunkenly. "I, Bgr the Chinger, was Elliot Methadrine all along!" Bgr thumbed his nose at the guy and gave a bronx cheer. The entirety of the bar applauded.

"What!" blustered the squat, red-faced deputy director. "And who is this suspicious-looking guy?" He glowered at Sir Dudley.

"Your remarks are most repugnant, sir. I suggest you remove yourself at once. Or else . . ."

"Or else! You threatening me? Maybe you're a Chinger in disguise." He glowered about, recoiled in horror. "In fact—my God! Books. Look at all the books here . . . why, you're all Commupops, aren't you? Arrest them all, Troopers! And burn these books. Immediately. Bill, get out of that silly dress and help them, and I'll reduce your sentence to a month of KP."

Bill sighed. He looked at his friends. And then he looked at the Troopers and at Deputy Director Insufledor.

He pulled his newly cleaned and oiled blaster from its holster at the side of his leg, thumbed the lever to MAXIMUM DEATH FRY, and raised it.

"Don't do it, Bill," cozened Sir Dudley. "Insufledor is certainly expendable. But you would never forgive yourself if you wasted those Troopers. I have a better idea."

Sir Dudley boomed with energy, expanding and glowing until his Time Portal reached the ceiling. The frightened Troopers fired energy blasts at him, but he just laughed, absorbed the energy and grew larger.

Then struck!

There was an eye-blasting surge of light, and when they could see again the Time Portal was gone. Along with Insufledor and his Troopers.

Bill sighed. "He was a good old Time Portal, he was. Let's drink to his health."

His subconscious had decided for him. He reached out thirstily, picked up the huge mug of beer and drained it in three large gulps.

The alcohol—after more than two years off the hooch—hit him like a damp sock filled with a lead pipe over his head.

"New corollary to the Meaning of Life," he said, his words slurring already. "Life may not mean bowb, but it comes damned close!" He then pushed his glass forward. "Lemme have another one of those, Nancy."

"Sure thing, Bill," said Uncle Nancy. "Coming up."

"Hey, dude!" cried the voice of the AI in his ear, speaking although unbidden. "What happened to Da Boss?"

Bill sighed. "About what is going to happen to you. Sir Dudley, wherever you are—can you hear me? Do you think you can take this implant along with the others?"

A card appeared in midair, dropped to the table.

"*No trouble there, Bill. Enjoy yourself,*" it read.

There was a little ping and a tickle in Bill's ear and the implant was gone.

"Gee—Bill, that leaves just you and me. Have a last drink before I go. War is hell." Bgr emptied his glass.

Bill in happy response drained another mug of beer, and the soft sweet music of inebriation and oblivion was soon whispering its alcoholic tunes to him yet again.

He ordered another one and then hoisted his interesting foot up onto the bar.

"You know, Nance," Bill said.

"What, Bill?" said Uncle Nancy giving him another beer and sealing his alcoholic future.

"This ain't such a bad-lookin' foot after all. You know, I think a Trooper should be *proud* of his foot, no matter what."

"Damned nice foot if you asked me, Bill," said Uncle Nancy.

"Yeah." Bill sipped at his new beer, slowing down his intake and taking over a minute to finish the two Imperial pints it contained. "By the way, guys," he said. "I was just telling you what the Meaning of Life was—and for the life of me, I don't remember exactly what I said!"

"Simple enough, old buddy. You said that life just doesn't mean bowb."

"That's what you said, Bill," Bgr said from the doorway. "Makes sense, doesn't it? Be seeing you."

"You're really a Chinger and I got to do my duty," Bill rumbled, reaching for his blaster. But the door was empty. He sighed and breathed aloud what, someday, if he lived that long, would be inscribed on his tombstone.

"Barman. I'll have another drink."

ARTHUR C. CLARKE'S VENUS PRIME

by Paul Preuss

VOLUME 1: BREAKING STRAIN   75344-8/$3.95 US/$4.95 CAN
Her code name is Sparta. Her beauty veils a mysterious past and
abilities of superhuman dimension, the product of advanced
biotechnology.

VOLUME 2: MAELSTROM   75345-6/$3.95 US/$4.95 CAN
When a team of scientists is trapped in the gaseous inferno of
Venus, Sparta must risk her life to save them.

VOLUME 3: HIDE AND SEEK   75346-4/$3.95 US/$4.95 CAN
When the theft of an alien artifact, evidence of extraterrestrial
life, leads to two murders, Sparta must risk her life and identity
to solve the case.

VOLUME 4: THE MEDUSA ENCOUNTER
75348-0/$3.95 US/$4.95 CAN
Sparta's recovery from her last mission is interrupted as she sets
out on an interplanetary investigation of her host, the Space
Board.

VOLUME 5: THE DIAMOND MOON
75349-9/$3.95 US/$4.95 CAN
Sparta's mission is to monitor the exploration of Jupiter's moon,
Amalthea, by the renowned Professor J.Q.R. Forester.

*Each volume features a special technical infopak,
including blueprints of the structures of Venus Prime*